I0445546

Tooley Times: The Britney Greene Story
(Chapter Titles)

1. How Did I Get Here?
2. Fake People
3. What is Love?
4. Jordan's Child
5. Business and Pleasure
6. The Devil Wears Plaid
7. Shallow People
8. You Need Jesus
9. Like a Movie
10. The Backlash
11. Opportunity
12. Once You Go Black…
13. Epiphany
14. Business as Usual
15. The New Girl
16. The Perfect Storm
17. Gone
18. What Doesn't Kill You…
19. Class is in Session
20. Old Habits Must Die
21. Extrasensory Perception
22. Serendipity
23. Olympus Has Fallen

ABOVE ALL ELSE I'd like to thank my Lord and Savior, Jesus Christ, just for being who He is. This novel is dedicated to both my mother, Helen Tangie and my husband, Joseph Williams. Without either of them in my life guiding and loving me, I would be physically, emotionally, and/or spiritually dead—so thank you for loving my unlovable a**!

a Tangier Tale
PUBLISHING

Chapter 1: How Did I Get Here?

~1999 Present Day~

... Or better yet, how do I keep ending up here? It's sad when a hotel establishment becomes so familiar; you're on a first name basis with its staff. No, I am not a celebrity on tour, nor am I the 'briefcase type' going from city to city on business. No, see me... I am scum. I would have said I am a whore, or a slut, or even a prostitute, but some of them get paid for their shenanigans, whereas I actually lose money every time I wake up here.

The Vacation Inn has no central air system, it's a dejected excuse for a hotel, and it's an even bigger insult to the connotations of the word 'vacation', yet I find myself coming back at least once every other month since the past year. What can I say? I am a creature of habit. The only thing constantly changing about this situation is the guest I bring with me during my stays.

In my defense, I don't have a car and the Vacation Inn is walking distance from my apartment complex, as a result I've learned to tolerate its numerous deficiencies. It's also only seventy-nine dollars a night, which is a great price considering I live in the newly gentrified city of Tooley. Tooley just started having horrendous issues with inflation and that's something I'm not used to considering I was born and raised in Dumois. *Dumois is a poverty stricken neighboring city, known for its crime and low income housing areas.* As teenagers, the neighborhood kids would rent out rooms at this very hotel and throw drinking parties; since we couldn't exactly have the kind of fun we wanted living in our parents' homes. So yea, my history with this place runs deeper than my more recent sexual escapades.

On this particular visit, I wake up freezing and staring blankly at a moldy ceiling. I turn to lie on my side and my focus shifts to a half empty liquor bottle that was recklessly thrown down on the carpet the night before. I also spot my clothes and begin wishing I was clearheaded enough to walk towards them... I sure could use any warmth they'd provide me with right now; but still fairly intoxicated, I stay put. I'm extremely dizzy from the alcohol I overindulged in the night before; I have to get drunk before nights like these because for me, alcohol equals confidence. Alcohol is the reason I was able to ride the guy I just spent the night with like a porn star, without at all being concerned or insecure about my not so perky breasts and visible cellulite. I'm far from an alcoholic and rarely ever drink with the exception of nights like these, but I'm sure that I'm not the only one who consumes liquor for the same reasons Popeye consumed spinach. I become more confident, fierce, and desirable with every shot.

I look up at the identical bed next to mine and see my guest sound asleep and carefree. *Must be nice,* I think to myself. He didn't have to pay a dime for the fun night he just had. Whereas, I paid for his dinner, his gas, the alcohol, this room, and I was the submissive one doing everything imaginable under the sun to please him... All he had to do last night was show up and get hard. Truth be told, I'm not even rich! I can't afford to live on my own nor do I drive, and I'm currently living check to check. Yet for some reason after all my bills are paid, I use any excess money I can conjure up to fund these random exploits. I am however grateful that this guy at least helped me attain multiple orgasms and didn't just roll over and die after the first round like many others had done before him.

~One Week Earlier~

2

I met him a week ago at the Burger Royale restaurant across the street from my job. I was in line when I spotted him behind the counter. He was noticeably younger than me, but still above the legal age of consent. Even in his uniform I could see how cut his arms and chest were and I liked how his hair draped down to his face from the rim of his blue and white, Burger Royale hat. I knew I wanted him when our eyes met and he gave me a flirtatious smile as I approached his register. After an awkward ordeal of flirting (that caused him to mess up my order) and after my food was finally ready, I wrote my cell phone number on the back of my receipt and handed it to him. "*Call me.*" I mouthed boldly as I walked out of the fast food restaurant.

I'll be the first to admit I'm not the prettiest girl in the world, but I clean up fairly nicely when I wear makeup, dress to kill, and remember to suck in my stomach. Reality is I have unruly, thick, brown hair, uncooperative skin, I'm only 5'3" but weigh 165lbs, and although I don't look fat enough to stand out for my weight, I dread being naked and exposing my flabby stomach. The only good thing about being thick is I am blessed with a nice sized d-cup bust and a round juicy ass that hot guys tend to appreciate. I'm almost always sleeping with men that are way out of my league in the looks department, even though they constantly fail in both the personality and life departments. The bad thing about me having dated outside of my league almost my entire life is: I end up always overcompensating financially in an attempt to keep a man interested in me. By spoiling good looking men (because I feel like it is the only way to keep one), I've developed insecurities and extremely low self-esteem. As a result, I am probably the world's youngest sugar mama at age twenty-six.

One thing I've learned about men in all my years of living is generally, the more you cater to them the less likely they are to respect you and want to be in a committed relationship with you. Men don't want a sappy woman they don't have to work hard to attain, and even though I am aware of all of this, I still make the same mistakes over and over again. I'm broken, stuck on the same song like a scratched up record. They say insanity is repeating the same things but expecting different results, I say *damn right I'm insane!*

~1999 Present Day~

It was his nonverbal decision to sleep on separate beds. After we finished having sex, it was like a switch turned off in his head and he no longer wanted to be bothered with my mushy antics. It upset him when I started rubbing on his back and playing in his hair, he reacted as if I was a stranger interrupting him from a good night's sleep. So of course, being the amazing body-language-detector that I am, I got up and gave him his space by relocating to the spare bed in our twin room. I was a little hurt that he didn't object or fight for me to stay in the same bed; in fact, he started snoring like a baby five minutes after I got up.

Funny how things change because he was all about me days earlier, he called me 'baby' and 'beautiful', he couldn't stop blushing when he'd see me, and he held every door I stepped through. Unfortunately, silly, broken me became excessively clingy and turned him off any chance of taking our relationship further. Three days after we met I called him way too much for *anyone's* comfort. I also confessed to him I was in a relationship on day four, then on day five I cried and screamed at him over the phone for being just like 'every other man' because he wouldn't tell me he loved me. Honestly though, I might not be the only one in this situation with problems, because despite all my signs of obvious mental disorder, he still agreed to meeting up with me for last night's rendezvous.

4

Regardless of how much I want to, I actually can't blame him for any of my emotional wreckage. I am the one in a seemingly committed relationship, yet I'm meeting random men and drawing them into my crazy life with promises of fun, sex and being pampered. Then after the sex is done, I have the nerve to get sad when they don't want anything serious to do with me. I swear on my father's grave I haven't always been like this, I swear I was once sane early on in my life. I don't remember exactly when all these esteem issues came into play, but I do know this; Anthony Johnson was the first guy I felt used and destroyed by.

~1992 Flashback~

I was nineteen years old and Anthony was twenty-three at the time, I was a fairly good girl back then plus he had only been my second sexual partner. I was a lot thinner and prettier in my teens, smoother skin and I only weighed 140lbs. Although Anthony was better looking and more popular than me, I held my own and wasn't too far behind him in both areas. I was so sprung and in lust that I would actually bring packed lunches to his job at the mall almost every day. I loved the way he dressed and I felt like having him by my side upgraded my teenage social status. I did so much for him which at the time was very unlike me; prior to Anthony, I had never spent a dime on *ANY* man. I bought him an expensive ass Georgio Wackori (G-Wack) watch; which was trendy at the time and valued at four hundred and ninety-five dollars. I still can't believe he accepted, *and kept*, my costly gifts even though he insisted he wasn't the 'commitment type' and kept telling me 'all he wanted with me was to have a good time'. It took a year of me throwing myself at him and doing whatever he asked before I grew some kahunas and walked away from it all. And then, BAM! Six months after I ended things with him, he met and married another woman.

Don't get me wrong, I didn't really love Anthony; it's just that every action he took felt like a blow to my ego. We didn't have much in common, the guy was materialistic and extremely self-absorbed, but he did wonders in elevating my

5

social status. It's just hard for me to grasp that he gave that broad his heart and soul just six months after meeting her. I mean, the more he pushed me away the more I did for him, yet it all ended up being in vain. I replayed our relationship over and over for months after seeing his wedding pictures everywhere thanks to our many mutual friends. What was wrong with me? Why wasn't I good enough? After the break up I kept trying to pinpoint my faults, but to this day I am no closer to any answers than I was six years ago. You see, even though I didn't want to marry him, I wanted him to *want* to marry me... Does that make sense?

~1999 Present Day~

Snapping back to my current situation, I stare at Burger Royale boy from across the room and realize how beautiful he looks sound asleep. If I didn't have to be at work in an hour and a half I would get back in his bed and force him into a fifth round, unfortunately I had to get in the shower immediately if I didn't want to be late. I stagger towards my knapsack and grab a pair of flip flops, a towel from home, and my own toothbrush and toothpaste, (can you tell I'm experienced in 'hotel stays'?) I turn on all the lights not caring if I wake him, he's practically useless to me at this point. I don't expect anything from him, I can already tell regardless of everything I did for him the night before that he's the type of person who's all about himself. He probably won't even offer to give me a ride to work, even though he knows that I'll have to take a bus in this zero-degree weather.

I wear my flip flops in the shower place and turn the handle to the hottest temperature. I love showers; I can stay in one for hours at a time if it's hot enough. I've always taken scorching hot, steamy showers since I was a child. I remember my mother used to come in after me, feel all the heat and steam, then nag that I was boiling my skin cells... *whatever that meant*. When I got older and started talking back to her I joked, "Maybe my body is used to this kind of heat because I'm the devil". Momma Emma didn't find that funny at all.

6

"Can I join you?" I am brought out of my memory and startled by the deep voice coming from the door of the bathroom. I move the shower curtain to the side to see perfection in boxer shorts staring back at me.

"Good morning, Sunshine." I joke. "If I wasn't rushing to get to work I would definitely take you up on that offer... But I don't want to mess around and miss my bus."

"How 'bout I join you in there, we take our time, and I take you to work afterwards, your job is across the street from mine right?" Wow. I was shocked by his willingness not only to go another round, but to want to do something nice for me. Finally, I met someone who matched my libido and charitable nature.

"Yes it is." I sing.

"Ok then, here I come." He warns me while dropping his boxer shorts and revealing his beautiful, well-endowed penis. I giggle as I pull his 5'11" ass into the shower with me.

"DAMN!" He shouts as the sweltering hot water hits the skin on his back. He quickly turns the knob to a more tolerable temperature and we begin kissing.

We pull up to my job on time, I am grateful and also in serious lust with this guy.

"Wow you work here?" He gawks in amazement at the modern building.

"Yea." I smile a little proud. "I told you the first time we spoke I worked across the street from the Burger Royale."

"Yea but I had no idea across the street meant, across the street at Hogan & Wildes! That's dope as hell baby girl." He admits.

"Thanks," I am beaming. "Well I guess I'll email you when I get settled in the office," I say flirtatiously.

"Yea, yea... cool." He brushes off my advance, "Look, can I hold about twenty dollars? I'm trying to buy some weed when I get back around my way."

Wow, I think, the nerve of this guy to ask for money after I spent almost half my savings on his ass the night before. This is why he was being so nice to me all morning...

for drug money? Damn shame, because I was so close to falling for his bullshit. I reach in my purse and pull out two twenties. "Here." I say coldly.

"Damn baby, I only asked for twenty, but thank you!" He immediately turns the fake charm back on, flips his long hair out of the way, and then kisses me on my cheek.

"No problem… thanks again for the ride." I hop out of his paint peeled, 1980's Subaru extremely proud of my innuendo and make a mental note, for my own sanity, to leave Burger Royale boy alone for good!

Chapter 2: Fake People

~1999 Present Day~

I walk into the five-story, glass front office building completely dreading the next eight hours of my life. On a regular day I hate my job, but this hangover is making that detestation much more intense. As soon as I step foot through the double doors, I begin a mental countdown to my freedom. Every step forward causes an intense pain in my head, *literally*, because of the noise created from my heels connecting with the marble floor.

I should love my job; I work for one of the most prominent, full service law firms in North America; Hogan & Wildes, LLP. We practice everything from immigration to entertainment law, so annually there are millions of dollars being made right in front of me. Unfortunately, out of those millions I am barely making eleven dollars an hour, which is an improvement considering my starting pay was only eight dollars. There are a lot of places where my current salary would be considered sustainable, but here in the newly gentrified city of Tooley, Missouri, the cost of living is becoming unimaginable. I am at the bottom of the totem pole at this law firm, I don't make far from what the janitorial staff and mailroom clerks make; the only difference is I get to sit on the same floor as the firm's Partners. I am the assistant to the legal secretary of Attorney William J. Hogan; basically that means I am the subordinate's subordinate. I am the hired help's, hired help. Ok... I think I've made my point. I flash my badge at security and walk past the reception area to the elevator lobby. I take one of the conveyors to the fifth floor/executive level where my desk is located.

Regrettably, the first person I see once the elevator doors open up is Evica Wildes. Evica is not only partner of this firm, but she has also been dubbed the wicked witch of the west side (since Tooley is west of Dumois). If life were a fairytale, I'd be waiting on a house to fall on her and finally end her dark reign. Evica was born and raised in Dumois; let me break down the significance of this. You see, Tooley is a fairly new city, in fact it used to be a part of Dumois twelve years ago until train tracks were built dead in the middle of the city dividing the upper/middle classes from the underprivileged. Buildings were torn down and rebuilt on the left side of those tracks and the newly cleaned up area was renamed Tooley. When I was growing up, there were no modern buildings in this city at all (especially none like the one this law firm is housed in), but now they seem to be popping up everywhere. Mom and pop shops are being replaced daily with mega businesses and major retail chains. Now walk about a mile east of those same train tracks and you'll find yourself in "old" Dumois, which is still decrepit, crime infested, and poorly funded by the government. My mother still lives in the same house I grew up in, in Dumois, but my fiancé and I moved to an apartment in Tooley a year after I got this job.

Evica used to be childhood neighbors with my mother, as in her family once lived directly across the street! Present day, Ms. Wildes acts as though she was born from a womb made of gold and looks down on anyone outside of her tax bracket. After Ms. Wildes attained her degree in United States Constitutional and Criminal Law, passed the bar, successfully defended a high-end area politician, and partnered with Hogan, it seems as though she suddenly developed amnesia and forgot her very humble beginnings. Please do not think I am jealous of her for bettering her circumstances and making it out of the projects. All I'm suggesting is, with all her

10

current successes it would be nice to see her giving back to the community she grew up in; whether financially or through mentoring. Especially since she had experienced firsthand how hard it was to grow up in such a deprived environment... But she doesn't give back... At all! Last year Ms. Wildes even turned down defending an elderly lady who had a hand in raising her because the woman couldn't afford the seven hundred and fifty dollars Evica charged, per hour, as a consultation fee. If that's not example enough of forgetting one's roots, then this should be: Evica was actually born Erica, but the financial gain allured her into changing the 'r' to a 'v' in an extremely sad attempt at sounding more exotic.

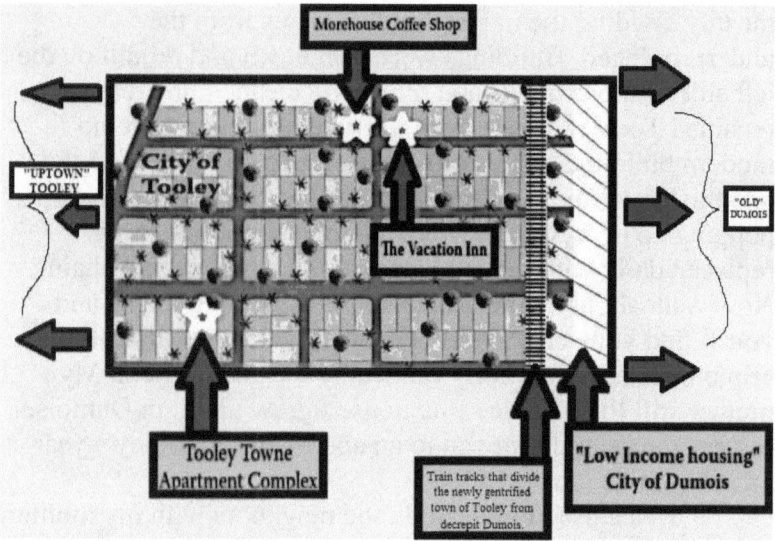

"Good morning!" She sings. "How was your weekend?"

"It was gr--" I start.

"Good, good, I left a list on your desk of things I need taken care of, since Louisa is running late. Be a darling and get that done as soon as possible." She flies by me, never even giving me a chance to respond to her initial question.

"*Bitch*", I speak under my breath after she is out of ears reach.

Louisa is always late. What else is new? The only reason she works here is because her last name is Wildes. Yes, that's correct... They are related. Louisa is the wicked witch's cousin. Word on the street is, the only reason Evica hooked this family member up with a job is because Louisa served time for her back in their teens. The cousins had been involved in a bank robbery which was committed in hopes of keeping up the illusion that they led a lavished lifestyle, and if it hadn't been for Louisa taking full responsibility and spending two years in a county jail, Evica would have never finished high school and gotten a college scholarship. Unlike her evil cousin, due to the ordeal, Louisa ended up not getting her diploma. She has a tenth grade education and can barely type two words a minute; yet... She's my boss. She also gets paid substantially more than I do, *but that's a different story*. There is about one legal secretary to every two or three lawyers at this firm, but because Louisa doesn't know diddly squat about the job, they hired an assistant for her; me. Together we both provide secretarial services to both William and Evica; the head honchos. Evica and Louisa are both now in their early forties with only a couple of months between them. Fortunately for her, Evica's money has been able to transport her face back to its mid-twenties. Aside from her horrendous attitude, she is beautiful, thin, tall, and very stylish, unlike her lumpy, short, heavy set cousin.

I sit at my desk, take off my coat, pour myself a cup of coffee, and then skim through the list Ms. Wildes has left me:

Number one: Make sure to get important package from Mr. Hogan and take it down to the mail room before noon.
Number two: Complete transcribing documents and prepare file for Douglas case.
Number three: Pick up my dry cleaning
Number four: Restructure my calendar how we discussed last week

Number five: File and organize the three boxes I have in my office under my desk.
Thanks darling, signed Evica.
I roll my eyes at the 'darling' and get to work.

     The door to Mr. Hogan's office must be more expensive than what my entire life is worth. It is made of solid wood imported from South Africa, with stunning hand carvings that effortlessly surround his gold overlaid name plate. I stand there a minute admiring the details in this luxurious door, as I often do, before I finally knock. I hear some quick scuffling on the other side of the door before a young blonde, whom I recognize from accounting, pushes through the door while adjusting her skirt. I look at her and scoff judging her by her obvious walk of shame, (even though hours earlier I had a walk of shame of my own leaving the Vacation Inn, I feel as though I'm better than her because I never mix business with pleasure). She avoids making eye contact and scurries past me, heading back to her department on the third floor.

     "Ms. Greene, come in." Mr. Hogan directs innocently.

     "Good morning Mr. Hogan, I didn't mean to interrupt. I was told to pick up a package from you." I speak as if I didn't just walk into a crime scene. Mr. Hogan was very much a married man, and Mrs. Hogan was not the blonde accountant I had just seen running out of his office.

"You're not interrupting a thing," He smirks "...And ah yes! The package Evica put together is right there, down in the credenza." He says pointing behind me. That's when I notice the undone button on his sleeve and the lipstick smudge on his collar. *Dog*, I think to myself. I swear this man kept everything 'in the credenza' in front of his desk. In order to get anything out of it, one would have to bend down in a compromising position which would give him a good view of their *ass*ets. I have been with Hogan & Wildes, LLP for three years now, so I am used to the blatant sexual harassment. I bend over hastily cutting his viewing time short and retrieve the package. I am trying to make my way out of his office quickly, at least before any rumors start up about me being his next chew toy.

"Britney," Mr. Hogan calls for me just when I am inches away from the door, "why are you always in a rush to leave my office?"

"No rush, Sir." I lie. "I just have a lot of work I'm trying to complete before the end of the day."

"Oh... well, may I join you when you decide to go to lunch?" He smiles menacingly, as if I didn't just witness the blonde woman before me stand in as his breakfast.

"Oh no, I'm not going anywhere special, I'm getting a salad across the street and coming right back to work." Way to hit that obvious advance out the park, I cerebrally pat myself on the back. If I had a dollar for every time I rejected Mr. Hogan, I would be just as rich as he is.

"Ok Ms. Greene, I'll let it go this time, but one of these days we'll get to know each other better." He shifts his focus towards his cell phone; I leave his office unfazed because this was our everyday dialog.

William J. Hogan is forty-eight years old, and despite my lack of sexual interest in him, he's a very handsome man. A towering 6'4', his presence alone commands respect. His neatly slicked back, salt and pepper colored hair is always very well retained. His life story is admirable, William is the son of an oil tycoon and unlike Ms. Wildes; his journey to the top was effortless. He was born into money so his parents were able to pay his way through law school. Unlike Ms. Wildes, Hogan studied entertainment law and became famous for representing some of the biggest celebrities in the country. He has an immense reputation for being a playboy and is rumored to fuck beautiful women of any status, from the biggest pop singers in the world to one of his cleaning ladies. After he made the Forbes list years back, women have been flocking to him despite his marital status. Nevertheless, I'm pretty sure his wife isn't bothered by the infidelity and keeps herself busy by spending her multimillion dollar allowance. I knew all this about him before I applied to work at his firm, and despite my sexual appetite I told myself from day one that I would never succumb to any of his advances.

Sometimes I feel like I am the only woman left in this office building that hasn't slept with Bill Hogan, even Evica and Louisa have been rumored to have had threesomes with him years before I got hired. His penis must be set on conquering everything in its sight, and that in itself is a major turn off. Although I am rather promiscuous, my legs do not spread with promises of advancement or for men in power. I also don't like to mix business with pleasure, and enjoy keeping my work reputation blameless and drama free.

I eagerly take the package down to the mailroom, which is located in the basement. The basement is not only where mail is processed and where the cleaning and building maintenance crews are located, but it is also home to vending machines. I am always excited to go down there because I cherish every opportunity to, not only get away from the egos on the fifth floor, but to enjoy a junk food splurge. Before I enter the mailroom I stop at a vending machine to get a snack. I straighten out a wrinkled dollar bill and attempt to indulge in some sugary bliss, but the machine eats my dollar and gives me no credit for it.

"FUCK!!!" I shout, ignoring my surroundings. I don't feel the need to watch my mouth, especially since no big wigs ever step foot down here. That was my last damn dollar! "I guess no honey bun for me." I pout.

"Need some help?" A young unfamiliar face comes out from the mailroom and startles me. He is probably the most handsome person I've ever seen in real life, *and mind you I've had my share of extremely handsome men.* He is wearing a mailroom uniform so I figure he must be the new clerk I heard some of the girls upstairs giggling about. I am mesmerized by his beauty. Although he isn't that much taller than me, he has a blemish free face and a hip young haircut that makes him look free spirited. He has hazel eyes, a wide contagious smile, his arms are covered in tattoos, and on top of all of that, he smells really, really good. "Here." He offers his assistance. He is strong enough to be able to tilt the machine and maneuver about three honey buns to fall out at once. Stealing honey buns from a malfunctioning machine can't be proper protocol, but I wasn't going to snitch. He hands me two of the honey buns and keeps one for himself.

"One is fine for me, thank you. I don't need any extra calories." I laugh awkwardly, handing him back one of mine.

"Really, are you calorie counting?" He asks.

"I don't know; I mean I'm already breaking my diet by eating one… And two honey buns don't make a right." I laugh.

"Well you look fine to me. Life is short; I say do what makes you happy." He smiles, and I can't tell if he's flirting with me or just always this friendly and engaging.

"You're right, but two honey buns can't be healthy for me." At this point I can't stop giggling and I don't know why.

"Ok, if you insist." He takes the honey bun from my hand. When his fingers brush against mine I feel a shock going through my entire body. My nipples instantly harden. "I'm Greg by the way." He reaches out his hand.

"Britney, Britney Greene." I shake his hand, another shock wave. "You must be new." I state the obvious attempting to distract my mind from all his sexiness.

"Yep, my first day was last Friday." He smiles feeling accomplished. "What do you do for the firm, if you don't

16

mind me asking? Judging by your nice threads, I'm guessing you're a lawyer?"

"Oh, I'm not a lawyer," I laugh "I only wear expensive looking skirt suits because I work on the fifth floor. I'm just an assistant to a legal secretary." I divulge.

"*Just?*" He teases, "Don't ever sell yourself short. Haven't you ever heard the story of the NASA Janitor?"

"No." I respond honestly.

"Well it's rumored that in 1962 John F. Kennedy visited the NASA space center and saw a man sweeping who was clearly a janitor. He interrupts his tour and goes over to the janitor, introducing himself and asks what the man was doing. Everyone with two eyes could see he was cleaning; he had a broom in his hands and some dusty clothes on. Nonetheless without missing a beat, the janitor responds enthusiastically 'Well Mr. President... I'm helping put a man on the moon'. Even though to the outside world he was only a janitor he realized his small role was essential to the overall success of the mission. Now I might have told the story incorrectly because it's been awhile since it was told to me, but the moral is still the same; No matter how small our roles are here we are contributing to the larger story unfolding in our individual lives, as well as the success of this firm. You know damn well there are hundreds of people in Tooley dying to get their foot in this very building... So working here, no matter what our positions are, is a big deal!" I am mesmerized by his drive and the passion in his hazel eyes.

"Wow, never thought of it that way." I blush.

"Yea, so you're not *just* an assistant to a legal secretary, and I'm not *just* a mailroom clerk."

"Got it!" I smile big, almost forgetting my reason for coming downstairs in the first place. "Oh! Speaking of mail room, I have a package I need to send out."

"Give it here, I'll run it for you."

"Aw, that's nice of you Gregory." I elongate his name as an awkward attempt at flirting... Okay I *really* need to work on my flirting.

17

"Ha! No problem Ms. Greene." He takes the package and walks towards the mail room, "It was nice meeting you." He winks and then disappears through the mailroom doors.

Greg is right, everyone and their mama wants to work and/or intern at this Law firm. It is the first of its kind in our state to reach this level of national success. Celebrities and respected politicians that otherwise would never make it to our small town in Missouri are constantly seen in our offices being defended by our immaculate lawyers. That's the only reason I've stayed here for the past three years making little to no money, the notoriety. I can't exactly move up in status sans a four-year degree or law school, and I only have a high school diploma. Also, since I'm on the fifth floor surrounded by millionaire lawyers, I am pressured into dressing the part minus the income. I am constantly skimming through thrift stores in search of second hand, brand name heels and designer suits. The amount of money I spend at thrift stores in order to keep up with my fashionable coworkers definitely adds to my financial distress. Every morning when picking out an outfit I can hear Evica Wildes' voice in my head, "Dress for the job you want, not the job you have", which is something she told me when I first interviewed with her years ago wearing an awful, outdated, oversized sweater. I ended up throwing that sweater away as soon as I got home, and completely changing my wardrobe. I guess now I'm just living by her advice and faking it 'til I make it.

Chapter 3: What is Love?

~1999 Present Day~

       After an hour long bus ride I finally arrive back home to my little Tooley Towne apartment... And to my fiancé. I know, I know, sometimes I forget I'm in a relationship myself. I open the front door and feel ecstatic to be able to take my heels off. Jeremy is sitting at his desk in the corner of our living room, I can see him working away from the doorway. Although our apartment isn't a studio apartment it is so small; it's like one big room sectioned off. It is probably one of the few remaining buildings in Tooley that hasn't been reconstructed, which is why the rent here has been fairly manageable. Jeremy and I don't care about the limited space, we're just happy to be away from the violence and poverty in Dumois. He gets up from his desk when he realizes I'm home, kisses my forehead, and then takes my bags (from my overnight hotel stay) into our bedroom.

       "Hey Babe." He smiles while returning from the bedroom. Jeremy seems ever so happy to see me; he gives me the coziest hug ever. His arms have always made me feel secure and loved.

       "Hey Daddy." I kiss him, equally excited and relieved to finally be home.

       "How was your St. Louis business trip?" *Business trip?* I almost forgot I had lied to him about being in St. Louis with Evica in order to be able to spend Sunday night with Burger Royale boy.

       "Oh, it was great." I awkwardly reply. Attempting to avoid him asking me any follow up questions, I rapidly change the subject, "Did you already eat? Would you like me to cook?"

       "No baby, I already cooked. I knew you'd be exhausted so I took care of dinner." He gets up to fix me a plate, "Go change out of those work clothes and relax." He suggests. I literally have the most caring man in the world by my side, he has a huge heart, and I really don't deserve him.

~1995 Flashback~

I met Jeremy Rogers at a cousin of mine's wedding; we were both twenty-two at the time. He was the hired DJ for the reception and I was wasted out of my mind. Remember, I only get drunk when I am on an operation to recruit potential sexual partners... And boy was I on a mission that night. I was so depressed from witnessing the bride and groom's happiness; I wanted to find a random guy to take me home and help fill my void. Unfortunately, I was related to most of the guys at the wedding, and the few attractive men in attendance that I wasn't related to were there with their other halves. I had given up on my search for a one-night stand and found an unoccupied table in the corner of the room. Once the reception had ended, a few family members stayed to help the newlyweds tidy up the venue. Of course my mother volunteered to help, being the annoyingly perfect angel that she is, but I was too drunk to be of any use and was ordered by her to take several seats. One of my mother's church friends had given us both a ride to the wedding so I had no other way of getting home and was forced to wait for the both of them to finish. I was also too drunk to take a bus, plus I'd look crazy wearing this fancy dress and boarding public transportation. I remember putting my head down to assist in stopping the room from spinning and five minutes after that an average looking, skinny guy tapped me on my shoulder and asked me if I was okay.

"I'm a big girl." I said rudely, exasperated with the lack of hot male options at the wedding. I hated going places like that with no available men, I wanted to leave immediately, but I had no choice but to wait.

"Okay, not to pry or be rude but I've noticed you've had quite a few drinks and you've been stumbling across this venue all night." I became irritated that this random guy was trying to give me a lecture on my drinking.

"...And?" I scoffed.

"And my brother died from someone crashing into him that didn't care about how much alcohol they consumed

20

either." I could see the pain in his eyes and felt bad about being so rude. I thought he was a creep for watching me drink all night, but I realized he was probably just genuinely concerned for my safety. The fact that he might actually be a good guy is what sparked my initial interest in him, he was really different. It also helped that the more I looked at him the more handsome he became. I especially liked his curly, jet black, bushy hair. I started imagining what my fingers would feel like running through his mane.

"Well… I'm not driving. I came here with my mother and her friend, but I honestly don't want to leave as late as they plan to." That's when the idea came to my head to ask him for a ride home. Who knows, it might even be fun! *What if this average man can actually throw down in the bedroom?* I thought to myself. "When are you ditching this joint?" I naughtily smirk, implying that I wanted him to take me home with him.

"I'm just waiting for my payment and then I'll leave. By the way, I'm the DJ, and my name's Jeremy."

"Jeremy, don't you want to take me home with you?" I persisted, this time winking so he would get the hint.

"I don't mean to be rude, but won't your mother worry about you going home with a stranger… Especially as drunk as you are?" He asked a little bothered by my blatant willingness to surrender myself to him.

"No, she doesn't give a shit about me." The alcohol made me exaggerative, loose lipped and bold.

"First of all, that's your mother, show a little more respect. Secondly, I'd be happy to take you to *your* house but I don't bring random women home to mine." *Wow*, I had never been turned down before, especially dressed like I was. I was wearing such an elegant form fitting gown, and the full body spandex suit I had on underneath helped give my body a false coke bottle shape; not to mention my cleavage looked AMAZING. I see that he was wearing glasses, but was this kid, blind? My make-up and nails were perfectly applied, and my hair was straightened and kept in a flawless up do with a couple of loose strands flowing down to my face. Who the hell did this guy think he was turning all this down? He must have seen the annoyance in my face because he immediately softened his approach.

"Look, you're a beautiful girl. You really are. I just wouldn't feel right taking you to my place because you deserve to be treated better than that. Here, drink this." He handed me a bottle of water, "And go home with your mom. I'm sure no matter what's going on between the two of you, it's fixable. I wish my brother was still around, no one has your back like family." With that he pulled out his business card and handed it to me. "My personal cell number is on that card; make sure you call me to let me know you got home safe." And that was that.

Of course I ended up not calling him. Despite how cute I thought he was, he was way too goody for me and had a fairly old soul. That responsible, adult act was a turn off; we were in our early twenties, nobody was thinking about family values and responsibility back then!

Six months after the wedding I had my heart broken by another handsome guy with bad intentions. He was one of those 'winners' in the looks department, but failed in every other category... especially in faithfulness. After I had sex with him he stopped returning my calls and I heard through the Dumois grape vine that he had gotten back with his ex-girlfriend behind my back. I must have just been his rebound, but still it hit hard because it had only been a year since I'd been played by Anthony Johnson. I remember crying all weekend and telling myself I was done with being used. While I was going through my messy purse trying to find a tissue-pack, I randomly spotted Jeremy's business card and finally decided to use it.

"Jeremy Rogers, speaking." He answered so business like.

"Relax I'm not a client," I joked, attempting to hide my nasally sounding voice that would give away the fact that I'd been crying.

22

"Wedding girl?" He asked. Wow, this kid was good. It had been six months since we met but he still remembered me and my voice?

"How'd you know it was me?" I asked him feeling both shocked and flattered.

"Well I only give my number to clients and I was actually really worried about you when you didn't call me that night, young lady. Plus, you're not exactly forgettable, that night your breath smelled like a mixture of liquor and puke." He laughed.

"SHUT UP!" I giggled.

"Anyways, great to hear from you Ms...?"

"Ms. Greene, but you can call me Britney."

"Nice to formally meet you, Britney."

"Likewise, Mr. Rogers." I smiled, because at that moment something inside me told me this guy was the real deal.

That night we talked for hours. I eventually broke down and told him everything about my life up until that point. I told him about the jackass that used me as a rebound, the issues I had with my mother, I touched on the 'Anthony Johnson' story, and I was honest to him about my issues with self-esteem, alcohol abuse, and sex. What I loved about speaking with Jeremy is that he didn't judge me, in fact, that night he actually prayed for me over the phone for about an hour. Fast forward to four years later, and here we are living together, and engaged! He proposed with no diamond, promising he would get me the ring of my dreams as soon as he was financially able, and I agreed, knowing that one day he'd be great.

Years later he remained a good guy, and now that rare, amazing man is in the kitchen fixing me dinner. In the beginning of our relationship it was almost as if he was too good to be true. He would never lie or cheat, and that made me hell-a suspicious. To me, nobody could be as perfect and as faithful as he appeared. I had been in my share of horrendous relationships so I knew from experience how to check for signs of someone cheating. But for four years

Jeremy's phone had never received a suspicious incoming call, I would even go through his phone records and never see anything suspicious, I would look through his bank statements and not find anything, I would follow him in cabs to events and he was always where he said he would be, with who he said he'd be with… Surprisingly he passed every one of my tests! It took me a while before I started believing he was just genuinely a good guy that lived a normal mundane life. So now, I completely trust him with all my heart, I always wish I could be that good for him.

Jeremy is brilliant, and although he graduated with high honors from the University of Missouri and could have gotten a senior level position at any of the new businesses popping up in Tooley, he followed his heart and took the harder entrepreneurship route. My fiancé started his own DJ company; Bells Will Be Ringing, LLC, when he was just twenty years old. Through years of intense labor, he literally built something out of nothing and managed to raise the money to attain the most expensive, high quality DJ equipment in our city. He genuinely enjoys what he does and is passionate about it. His work ethic and integrity are unmatched and that's exactly how he attains most of his patrons. Everyone he DJs for ends up recommending him to other clients. He is legitimately doing very well for himself and his business is growing daily. He makes a little more than I do and even though we can't afford a house right now (because we've invested most of our money into his trade), I have faith in the businessman that he is and know that any day now we'll be living luxuriously.

~1999 Present Day~

"Mm… Smells so freakin' good in here! What's for dinner?" I come into the kitchen after changing into some house clothes.

"Shrimp linguini." He announces very proud of himself handing me a plate. I dig in and it tastes AMAZING… almost as amazing as he is.

After dinner we both are in bed. He is fast asleep and facing the wall. Lately our sex life has been nonexistent. We are both hard workers and by the time we get to bed we're both extremely exhausted; plus, to be honest I've never been too attracted to the 'good guys'. I love Jeremy and know he has a big heart, but sexually, I am a devious masochist, only turned on by men that emotionally scar me.

While lying in bed my mind suddenly shifts from how I met Jeremy to how much I want to get to know Greg from work. I start replaying the entire conversation we had by the vending machines and my nipples start to harden. I feel my body yearning for him as my thoughts wander; I would *love* to taste his lips. I start to think about him so hard I can smell his cologne. At this point I am so freaking horny I'm debating waking Jeremy up and using him for his penis, even though Greg is really who I am thinking about this very moment. Immediately I feel guilty about even considering playing Jeremy like that, so I end up letting him sleep. It takes me two hours to finally fall asleep, and when I do, I start to dream:

I am at the vending machines again, this time wearing nothing but a silk robe. Greg comes out of the mail room looking like a Greek god. All he has on are boxer shorts. His

25

tatted body is glistening and I can see from the rise in his shorts that he wants me as much as I want him.

"Britney, damn baby girl I've missed you." He runs towards me and holds me so tight I melt in his arms. He loosens my robe and exposes my all natural d-cup breasts and erect nipples. He starts to caress each one tenderly and sends shock waves from my chest to my groin area. I moan with gratification but the moans are silenced when he starts to tenderly kiss my lips. "I've wanted you since the first time I saw you." He confesses hungrily, as he moves his mouth from my lips to my neck. "I've wanted to taste every part of you." He continues down to my breasts. He starts to lick and tease each nipple until I can't take it anymore. I grab his head and force my left nipple deeper into his mouth, until his lips are covering my entire areola. I feel his tongue dance circles around my nipple and my body loses control, I faint in his arms from pleasure. He guides my tranquil body to the floor with his lips now around my right nipple and I simultaneously slip entirely out of my robe. He stops for a minute and looks at me as if he's examining a piece of art, as if my 'real woman' curves didn't bother him. "Damn you're so beautiful." He coos.

"So are you." I exhale staring deeply into his hazel eyes. His kisses go from my nipples to my stomach. I'm normally insecure about my mid area, but he plants the most sensual French kisses all over my stomach and he's being so gentle, loving, and passionate with me that I forget I have stretch marks and love handles. When he gets to my belly button, I wrap my legs around his shoulders. "Please Daddy, taste me." I beg him as he purposefully moves slower on his southern route. Then just when I can't take it anymore, and without warning, I feel his tongue hit my clit and I begin to lose my mind. I start grinding my hips against his tongue and lips and feel myself becoming extremely wet. He then turns animalistic and proceeds to eat my pussy as if it's made out of liquid caramel. I can't take it anymore; I reach down towards his boxers and become senseless by the feel of his warm, extending dick. "Please daddy put it in." I beg as I

26

stroke on his member impatiently. I start feeling a little wetness on my fingertips coming from the head of his penis, further causing me to lose my mind.

"You ready Baby?" He pants, adrenaline flowing through both our veins.

"Yes baby, please." I squirm with anticipation. He stands up and takes his boxers off. He spreads my legs and teases the entrance of my pussy with his now fully extended penis. Just when he is about to thrust his big dick inside of me for the first time...

...My alarm goes off and it's now time for me to get up and get ready for work.

Chapter 4: Jordan's Child

~1999 Present Day~

Louisa is three hours late... What else is new? It's close to noon and I've already completed most of the day's work, so it really wouldn't affect me if she decided not to show up at all. I've been rushing through tasks all morning in attempt to stay busy because ever since I had that dream about Greg last night, he's been consuming my thoughts. Usually when I start obsessing over a guy like this, inevitably I sleep with him. The problem with this situation is he works with me and I have a strict rule against fucking co-workers; hence my dilemma. Why did he have to be so damn fine and smell so damn good? Why did he have to be so damn charismatic and be covered in those sexy ass 'bad boy' tattoos? Just then, I feel a hand on my shoulder that startles me out of my dirty thoughts.

"Good morning, Ms. Greene." William Hogan sings as he continues to massage from my neck to my elbow.

"Good morning, Mr. Hogan." I respond hunching forward towards my desk so my shoulder is no longer within his reach.

"Louisa's out again?" He sighs with disappointment, and I'm not sure whether it's because he's really annoyed by Louisa or with the fact that I moved my shoulder.

"No, I think she's just running a little late." I inform him.

"Please send her to my office when she gets here, I don't know who she thinks she is, but she can't continue to just show up whenever she wants." It's about time he notices Louisa's lack of concern for her job. It's not fair that I bust my ass every day while she's out shopping with her much bigger salary.

"Yes sir, will do." I reply knowing damn well that whatever trouble Louisa is in, Evica will inevitably find a way to bail her out of it.

"What are we doing for lunch today, Britney?" Mr. Hogan asks, completely changing the subject. I swear this man never gives up.

"Mr. Hogan, I only have a thirty-minute lunch break." I utter while subconsciously rolling my eyes, "You know I don't drive so I have to run across the street, order something fast, eat it on the way back, and then be back at my desk in time punch in. Lunch with me wouldn't be exciting." I share, hoping it will set him straight once and for all.

"What if I make it an hour lunch? Would you eat lunch with me then?" He bargains.

"Mr. Hogan--"

"Call me Bill."

"Uh... Mr. Hogan, I just... I just can't." I say exasperated.

"Ok, ok. I get it." He sounds defeated and begins drifting back towards his corner office like a sad dog with its tail between its legs. Damn... He is such a persistent mother fucker, *excuse my French,* but it is starting to make me feel very uncomfortable. I know that the only reason he's interested in me is because I'm fresh meat. I'm the only woman in this building he hasn't sunk his teeth in yet and it's driving him crazy. All that rejection I just had to exude made me hungry, thankfully as I look down at my watch I realize it's officially lunch time.

Despite what I told my boss, I didn't actually plan on going to any fast food restaurant across the street for lunch. Not only because I've been avoiding the Burger Royale like the black plague, but I actually have an intense craving for vending machine snacks... *if you catch my drift.* I punch out for lunch and take about three dollars out of my wallet and make my way down to the basement in hopes of another encounter with the current man of my dreams.

I put all three dollars into the machines and pick out an orange soda, a bag of chips, and a bag of mixed nuts. I spend about ten minutes of my lunch lingering around the basement hoping to see Greg, but he never comes out of the mail room. Impatient, I decide to peek through a glass window that overlooks the room to see if he is even at work today. I creep over to the glass and slightly bend down in a way to avoid being seen by anyone on the inside. When I look through the glass I see something that makes me extremely jealous and angry. Greg is sitting on a counter eating a sandwich and the same blonde girl from accounting that was in Mr. Hogan's office the day before, is sitting in a chair next to him. She looks pathetic, and although I can't hear their conversation, she appears to be laughing a little too hard at almost everything he is saying. I am so livid I forget to continue ducking and stand straight up. Greg catches sight of me and I give him a deathlike glare. I don't care that he sees me; at this point I'm officially over him and could care less about impressing him. He is just like every other guy in the world, nothing special about this one, just another Anthony Johnson. I storm past the vending machines and press a button to call an elevator to take me back upstairs. I can't believe I wasted thirteen minutes of my lunch on that douche bag.

"BRITNEY!" I hear Greg calling for me. I start to press the elevator button harder hoping one will arrive soon.

"What?" I respond irately.

"What's up girl? You mad at me or something?" He looks confused after he hears the bitter tone in my voice.

"Well, I was going to say hi, but I saw you were having a grand old time with Blondie and didn't want to interrupt." I say as sarcastic and as rude as I can.

"Ha! Who Jane? No, she's just cool peoples. She was introducing herself, that's all. Still don't know anyone in the building so I'm just making new friends. But I was actually hoping to see you today." He says exactly the right words, and sounds so genuine saying them.

"Why were you hoping to see me?" I smile, flattered. He is slowly melting the ice that once surrounded my heart.

"Because I really liked talking to you yesterday." My stomach instantly fills up with butterflies.

"Well... I only have about five minutes left on my lunch break. So I can't exactly talk now." I say after looking at my watch.

"Oh ok. Well where did you park? I could meet you in the garage when you get off and we could catch up for a little bit before you head home."

"I can't. I don't drive, and my bus will leave me if I don't leave here at 5PM sharp." I honestly reveal.

"Oh well even better," He says unfazed. "Meet me on the second floor of the parking garage when you get off, and I'll give you a ride home. Where do you live?"

"About an hour bus ride from here, I live in those Tooley Towne apartments." I disclose.

"Oh ok, that's a bet!" As soon as he ends his sentence Jane AKA blonde girl from accounting turns the corner, she must feel some type of way having been left alone in the mail room because disappointment is written all over her face. The thought of her sitting in the cramped area by herself for the past couple of minutes while he ran after me makes me ecstatic. She gives me a cold look and then turns to Greg.

"Well Greg, it was nice meeting you, I'll probably be back down here at one tomorrow, is this what time you normally take your lunch?" She speaks completely ignoring my presence and the fact that Greg and I were in the middle of a conversation of our own.

"Actually Jane, I'm going to be really busy the rest of this whole week with backed up packages so most likely I'll be working throughout my breaks." Greg informs her. In my head I am doing back flips. I honestly don't know how truthful he was being to her but it didn't matter. She wasn't going to have lunch with him all week and I couldn't be happier.

"O... K..." She sounds so annoyed and I love it. Just then, one of the elevator doors opens up and Jane gets in first.

"So I'll see you after work, right?" Greg confirms with me. I immediately nod yes. "Remember, I'm parked on the second level." He adds.

"Yea, of course, see you then." I croon, loving the fact that Jane is here to witness the end of our conversation as we're sealing up plans to meet up later. I get into the elevator with her and the door closes on Greg waving at me and me blushing harder than I ever have in my entire life.

Louisa is at her desk when I arrive back at mine.

"Girl did you tell Hogan I was running late?" She asks irritated.

"He wanted to know where you were... So I told him." I reply honestly. I wasn't going to lie for her anymore like she used to make me do in the past.

"Well I just got out of his office and he said I'm going to get written up for this shit. I swear to God wait 'til Evica comes back in." I am too 'in heaven' to pay any attention to Louisa and her ghetto fabulous neck snaps. Just then the phone on my desk rings and it's Mr. Hogan.

"Hello?" I answer.

"Ms. Green, can you please come to my office?" He instructs, and then hangs up. *Okay...* What the hell was that about?

"Where are you going?" Louisa skewers noticing I am walking towards Hogan's office, "Didn't you snitch on me enough for one day?" Ignoring her ignorance, I continue my route to Hogan's office and knock on the beautiful wooden door.

"Come in." He calls from his desk. I open the door and see him typing on his computer and notice he has a lot of thick books spread all across his desk. He must be working on an important case, so what could he possibly want with me?

"Yes sir?" I ask confused.

"It's come to my attention that you've been seen having inappropriate encounters with our new mailroom attendant, Greg?"

"Ha! And who brought that to your attention, Jane from accounting?" I laugh at how dumb this situation was.

"My source isn't important; I just have to make it clear to you what our employee guidelines are when it comes to kissing co-workers."

"KISSING?" That came out way louder than I intended it to, "I didn't kiss Greg." I spat.

"Well that's just the thing, when you're seen frolicking with employees that aren't even in your department, rumors like that start. So just do yourself a favor and keep it professional while you're in my building." He commands.

"Look Mr. Hogan, I didn't kiss anyone! And you calling me in here for something so petty can be viewed as borderline harassment. You should know better than anyone I don't mix business and pleasure." I say throwing a slight jab at his ego.

"Ok, I believe you. Just be careful." He gives me a fake smile before looking back down at his paperwork. I wasn't about to just let this go, Jane started this and I'm going to finish it.

"Well since Jane is so worried about who I'm kissing; did she tell you the reason she saw who I was with was because she was in the mailroom her damn self?" His eyes look back up at me quickly, "Yep, she was giggling like a little school girl at everything Greg was saying." After I drop that bombshell on Mr. Hogan's lap, I turn around and storm out of his office before he can even respond. I made my point and I know it will eat at him. If he was mad at me flirting with Greg, I'm pretty sure he is livid at the news of his little chew toy flirting with someone else. This building is occupied by mostly women fifty years old and younger and I'm pretty sure that's the work of Mr. Hogan himself. Greg slipped through the cracks becoming one of the only two men in the building worth looking at. Must be hard for Hogan to share the spotlight, definitely something he's not used to. Hopefully this jealous spurt was caused by the attention shift and really had nothing to do with me personally, either way, *Britney - 1, Jane - 0, don't come for me unless you're sent for*, I warned her telepathically.

Five O'clock couldn't have come any sooner. Plus, I am a little relieved I don't have to take a bus today with all this rumor bullshit on my mind. Jealous Mr. Hogan, Louisa accusing me of being a snitch, Jane being an actual snitch… It was all entirely too much.

I wait by the 2nd floor parking garage entrance for about a minute before I spot Greg. He is already by his car waving at me to walk towards him. It isn't the fanciest looking car, but at least it's in way better condition than Burger Royale's Subaru. I don't own a car so I'm not at all picky, anything is better than having to take that hour long bus ride.

Before I even get inside his car I yell, "Can you believe that little bitch Jane told Mr. Hogan I kissed you today on my lunch break?"

"What?" He says in disbelief. "That's kind of psycho on her part that she would start that rumor." He continues while he unlocks my door.

"Yea… Look, if you've got something going on with her, please don't put me in the middle of that shit because I've been drama free for the past three years."

"You got it woman, I don't want any drama either." He laughs and starts the car, "I just got to make sure not to be so friendly with people whose characters I'm unfamiliar with."

The conversation on the rest of the ride home has nothing to do with work. We talk about everything from politics, to religion, to goals, and we laugh so hard my sides hurt. He is smart and funny and has such a calculated view of the world; I am really enjoying my ride home. When we finally arrive at Tooley Towne my heart sinks at the thought of it all coming to an end.

"Wow you live in Tooley?" Greg asks in disbelief. "We were driving so close to the tracks; I was thinking you were in Dumois like me."

"Oh, no… I moved out here a couple of years ago. It's not as nice as uptown Tooley where the office building is, but it's affordable."

"No this is nice… I can't wait to move out my damn self. Any ways, this was fun. Do you want to call me?" He says brushing his finger across my cheek. He can see it in my face that I don't want to leave him. I nod and he motions for me to take out my phone. "988-0953." He recites, I type the number in my phone and save him as a new contact. "Are you going to use it?" He asks.

"I don't know... Things are complicated right now. But thanks for the ride." I sigh as I start to exit his car.

"Wait, Britney..." He stops me as I'm climbing out of the car and as soon as I turn to face him, his lips are on mine. *Am I dreaming again?* I think to myself. This has to be a continuation of the dream I had last night! Despite what I keep telling myself this kiss is real, we are really kissing. I feel his soft, yet firm lips kiss me passionately for the next five minutes. They taste just like I had dreamed they would. I want so much more than to kiss him, but we are right outside of my apartment complex and I can't risk Jeremy stumbling upon us.

"That was amazing," I catch my breath as he finally frees my mouth, "but I really have to go." I say abruptly and in a panic.

"What's wrong? I told you I wouldn't let the drama get at you. We can keep us a secret at work." He genuinely confirms.

"It's not just the 'at work' drama, Greg... I'm engaged." I admit.

"Really?" He looks at my ring finger surprised at the absence of a diamond.

"We just can't afford the ring right now." I honestly inform him.

"Oh." He replies which turns the conversation awkward.

"I'm sorry, I got to go... but see you at work, and thanks again!" And with that I jump out of the car, slam the passenger door shut, and sprint towards my building.

Thankfully when I walk in the door Jeremy is in deep concentration working with his turntables. I feel so relieved. Even though I've cheated on Jeremy frequently, I don't ever want to know how he'd react if he ever found out.

It's now bed time and before I fall asleep I keep thinking about my current situation. I am genuinely interested in two men at the same time. I have never felt like this since Jeremy and I made it official. I always just use the men I cheat on Jeremy with for sex and never really like, or see myself with any of them. I feel like Greg is different; I want him more than sexually. I want to be with Greg almost as much as I want to be with Jeremy... Shit!

I keep replaying how he stood up for me by the elevators with Jane, and how he chose me over her. Jane is a gorgeous girl, she's skinny, flat chested and has a really small ass, but her face is flawless... Plus she's blonde! Why would he ever pick me over her? Maybe he feels the same way I do. Maybe I consume his thoughts and dreams the same way he consumes mine.

"Babe." Jeremy startles me when he wakes up reaching for me to scoot in closer to him. For a second I thought I was thinking out loud and he overheard my confessions. I move closer to him and rest my head on his chest. He slowly drifts back to sleep and at that moment I feel extremely guilty for the first time. I feel guiltier for kissing and wanting to be with Greg than I've ever felt for having sex with all the men I've fucked behind my fiancé's back combined. Tears stream down my cheek and I quickly try to wipe them away before they hit Jeremy's chest. I start hating myself. This man deserves someone better than me, someone honest who won't hurt him, but I can't just let him go, because... I'm selfish.

I don't know why throughout the years I've become so promiscuous. I read some books and magazine articles by people who are just as promiscuous as I am and have always tried to find the root of my sex addiction. Most of the other people I read about were sexually abused as children and/or were raised in violence; neither of those circumstances described my childhood. I was never abused, I was never mistreated, yet I turned out just like my father who was never really around.

My father was a rolling stone; wherever he laid his hat was his home. *Yes*, like the song. He emotionally scarred my mother and would never show her respect. He would always cheat on her until she toughened up one day and filed for divorce when I was about six years old. Even then, I was not exposed to any violence or drama. They were always careful to shelter me from all their baggage. It wasn't until after I developed my obsession with men that I started connecting the dots between how similar my father and I are. He died of AIDs when I was twelve years old, so hopefully we don't end up too similar. R.I.P. Jordan Greene, gone but not forgotten.

Chapter 5: Business and Pleasure

~1999 Present Day~

I am sitting on a toilet seat inside of a stall, texting and playing a game, when I hear the voices of a group of women entering the bathroom. I don't recognize any of the voices at first, which isn't unusual being as though I am on the third floor. This is my regular hiding place for hectic days like these, I use restrooms on different floors to avoid running into the two causes of the majority of my headaches; Louisa and Evica. I actually don't need to urinate, in fact my pants are still on, I just need a couple of minutes alone to clear my head since work is taking such a mental toll on me. Today Evica left both Louisa and me a hefty to-do list to complete, but of course Louisa pretended to be sick and was granted permission to leave early. For that reason, I've been working like a horse all morning trying to pick up the extra slack.

The women that came into the restroom begin giggling profusely, I have no choice but to ignore my phone and listen in on their conversation, especially since they are causing such a commotion. "She's such a joke! I don't even see what Greg sees in her, I swear I look way better. He's probably just playing games with me to get me jealous." I overhear the first woman saying, and after putting two and two together I quickly realize that that woman is Jane, the blonde from accounting. I also figure out fairly quickly that she is talking about me. No one expects me to be using a third floor restroom since I'm stationed on the fifth floor, which is probably why Jane and her posse continue their loose lipped conversation buoyant of their surroundings.

"Definitely, you're way hotter than her, she's fat." A second woman laughs. I can't put a name to her voice but I'm sure if I see her I'll recognize her.

-**Hogan & Wildes, LLP** is a six story development (including the basement) with over five hundred employees; each floor is occupied by its own department. The basement, of course, houses the mail room, cleaning crew, building maintenance departments, and vending machines. The first floor houses the lobby/seating area for clients and the security station. The second floor is home to mainly the HR and marketing departments, with some runners here and there. The third floor, which I am on now, is where the accounting department is as well as our fully stocked, impressive law library, which is equipped with over seven adept librarians. The fourth floor is occupied by over a hundred paralegals, law clerks, legal assistants, and investigators, and the fifth and final floor is where a handful of the company's biggest bread winning attorneys, *and their secretaries,* share office spaces with Bill and Evica. As a result of its dominion, the fifth floor is much nicer than any other floor and accommodates a gym and a beautiful greenhouse. Also, on every floor there are three enormous bathrooms with multiple stalls, fully loaded work areas, full kitchens, and lounge rooms with eighty-inch TV's. So realistically, there is no reason, *other than mine,* to be on any floor other than your own. It's not uncommon working here to only know the names of people in your department or floor. Also, in my three years here, I've noticed things tend to be very cliquey within departments, floors, and even pay grades.-

"I doubt Greg likes her, you make more money than Chubb's. Plus, she always walks around here like she's better than everyone just because she's on the fifth floor with Hogan and them. I think she belongs with the mailroom guy, she's just an assistant, and they probably make the same salary." Says a third, snootier voice.

"I don't care if he's a mailroom clerk or not, Greg is hot. You know I'm a sucker for gorgeous guys regardless of their status. Plus, he looks like such a bad boy with that haircut and those tattoos... I want him! I've never had a guy turn me down before either, so I like the challenge. He needs to be with me instead of her and I'm going to get him, watch! In a week he'll be all over me." Jane speaks ever so confidently. The three women proceed going back and forth, dragging my name for filth. They are laughing so hard; I even hear Jane start to snort uncontrollably. At this point I am sick to my stomach and have had enough of their bullshit. I proceed to flush the toilet I was sitting on even though nothing made it into the bowl. After the flush I immediately hear all three girls begin to shush each other, I guess they finally realize they aren't alone in the bathroom and become extremely quiet. I am fuming as I exit my stall and walk straight towards Jane and the other two women who suddenly turn pale at the sight of me.

"Oh, don't stop on my account." I spew venomously. "My momma always said 'you know you're doing something right when they talk about you', so I know I must be winning." I emphasize as I intentionally pick and walk over to the sink closest to where the girls are standing. I stop at the sink, turn it on and take my sweet time fixing my hair while the three women just stand there slightly frightened. I think they sense, especially with our differences in size (me being a size twelve and all three of them being size zeros) that if one of them says the wrong thing I will mop the floor with all their faces. It is gratifying watching each of them look so awkward and uncomfortable, you can cut the tension with a knife. One thing I am not afraid of is confrontations, when someone treats me shady they'll get double the shade in return. I remember always getting suspended in high school for fighting for this very reason. This is why I don't trust or get along with other women. "And for your information," I continue my attack as I fold up my sleeves and begin to wash my hands, "Not that it's any of y'all God damned business, but the reason I'm not fucking William Hogan or Greg from the mailroom is because I'm engaged. And you'll be good to know that my fiancé adores my *chubby* ass. And honestly even if I wasn't in a relationship, I have enough self-respect to *not* mix business and pleasure, and that's something all three of you bum bitches lack. And I don't give a fuck how much more your salaries are, the truth remains that class cannot be bought." After I get all of that off my chest and make myself extremely clear, I treat the bathroom tile like a runway and stomp my heels, with extra attitude, as I make a grand exit.

I get back to my desk feeling like I've just been in a boxing match. My heart is racing, and even though I'd won that spar, it really hurt me that my name was being slandered. If Jane wants Greg that bad she can have him. I haven't even used the number he gave me yesterday when he dropped me off. I was going to go visit him during my lunch break and thank him again for the ride home, but after the incident I just endured I think its best I keep my distance. As beautiful as that man is he is not worth all this drama.

"Bill needs you in his office." Evica's voice startles me.

"Oh... ok." I respond warily. The last time I was called into Mr. Hogan's office it was for some rumor Jane started about me kissing Greg. My stomach turns at the thought of this being about what just went down in the ladies' bathroom. If I lose my job over this bullshit I will be meeting that blonde bitch outside.

"Your name's been coming up a lot in meetings recently." Evica smirks, while flipping her perfectly layered hair extensions, "You must be making a hell of an impression on Bill." She continues. I know exactly what that witch is suggesting, implying that I have been spreading my legs for the sudden recognition. If she had been Jane I would have already punched her square in the mouth, but she isn't, she's my boss's boss, so I keep my composure and just quietly get up and head down to Mr. Hogan's office.

I have no idea why Mr. Hogan is suddenly on 'team Britney', this out of the blue concern he now has for me is noxious. He's only now, after three years of working my ass off, bringing me up in 'big wig' meetings? He's now suddenly worried about who I'm kissing? I don't know what exactly is going on here, but it needs to stop! Standing outside of his beautifully carved door I begin mentally preparing myself for how I was going to politely tell the man (who signs my checks) to back the fuck off. I raise my arm, but before I even get the chance to knock, I hear Bill calling me from inside of his office.

"Ms. Greene?"

"Yes." I respond slightly irritated.

"Ooh good, come in." I take a deep breath then turn the knob and walk in. Internally I am so angry, I have my fists scrunched up and I'm taking very slow deep breaths to calm myself down.

"Look Mr. Hogan..." I begin.

"Bill." He corrects me for the thousandth time since I've worked here. That's when I notice a bottle of champagne and two flute glasses on his desk.

"See, I'm glad you called me in here because this is exactly the kind of stuff I need to talk to you about..." I lose my composure. A smile creeps on Mr. Hogan's face as he stares at me with wide eyes as if surreptitiously mocking me. "I get talked about enough as it is and my name comes up all over this building, Jane must have it out for me, I already know what this is about. Mr. Hogan..."

"Bill." He reiterates.

"I call you Mr. Hogan because you are my boss. We are not friends, we are not lovers, and if you weren't the owner of this law firm I would have already reported your various advances to HR. I shouldn't be called to your office for non-work related issues and I most definitely should not be coming up in important meetings!" I shriek. As I wait a while for my millionaire boss to respond I am irritated about how nonchalant he appears. Without making so much as a peep, he reclines in his chair and gives me a wide grin as if to say *you're so cute*. "What is so funny?" I ask with heavy attitude. A pet peeve of mine is when I am at the brink of tears and the person I am quarreling with takes me for a joke.

"Well Ms. Greene, nothing is funny, I've heard everything you've said and I'll definitely work on making Hogan & Wildes a more professional atmosphere for you." He smiles, "But Britney, I honestly didn't invite you in my office to talk about any drama with Jane, and this is very much work related. I've been bringing your name up in meetings because; as you know every year we are invited to an Annual Business Gala in DC. Due to our marginal successes this year, we are the ones being honored. I'm even going to be giving a speech… *AND* I would like to take *YOU* along." My heart stops. I just spent the last five minutes giving my boss's, boss's boss a piece of my mind, and all for nothing.

The Annual Business Gala in DC is a huge deal. There are cameramen, congressmen, prominent lawyers, doctors, entrepreneurs, celebrities, all kinds of business moguls in different avenues in attendance, there to network. It is solely on an invite only basis that one is able to attend this function, and your business has to be worth more than eight million dollars in order to make the guest list. Every year Bill is known for taking a secretary to this event instead of his wife. There are legendary tales of former secretaries that accompanied Hogan to the gala, and have come home millionaires themselves. A large percentage of the women he has taken with him in the past, now own successful businesses of their own. The amount of connects under one roof at that gala is amazing, someone in my position with the right networking abilities could potentially walk away from the experience with an investor, some great advice, and/or a higher paying job. The bad part of accompanying the biggest playboy in the world to this gala is; the incontestable exchange of a respectable reputation for undoubtable success. Yes, almost every secretary that has gone with Mr. Hogan is successful now, but they are also known across the country for sharing a hotel suite with the business world's most notorious sex symbol. Whether or not these poor women even slept with him doesn't matter, the rumors end up all over tabloids the next day and then they get labeled as a successful woman who obtained the world on her back.

"I'm confused." I almost choke on my words. "I… I'm not even your legal secretary. That's Louisa. I'm just her assistant."

"You're right." He confirms. "I only take *actual* legal secretaries, but since you've been so blatantly honest with me today, can I be just as honest with you?" I nod bashfully. "Louisa sucks at her job, Britney… You and I both know that. I've been trying to get rid of her for months; she's lazy and wouldn't be able to handle the demands of accompanying me at an event of this magnitude. The only reason she still has a job is because of her cousin Evica, but I have a plan; if you do a good job being my right hand at this gala, I will promote you to legal secretary and demote Louisa to being your assistant." I stand there in shock and take everything in before I muster up the courage to voice the concerns that are really on my mind.

"It sounds like an amazing opportunity but I don't want to sleep with you and end up in a tabloid, plus if you give me Louisa's job, she and Evica would hate me!" Mr. Hogan abruptly burst into laughter.

"Well damn! Is my reputation really that bad?" He jokes, knowing damn well he's known as the nation's whore.

"Yes. And the fact that some of the women even came out with tell all books about their night with you at past galas speaks volumes! *So* I just can't." I make my decision and am not budging. The opportunity sounds great but it isn't worth bringing shame to my family and hurting Jeremy. Plus, even though I dislike the Wildes it feels like a backstabbing move on my part to just take over as lead secretary.

"Eighty-five thousand dollars." Mr. Hogan smirks.

"What's that?" I ask confused.

"How much Louisa makes a year doing your job, and how much do you make now, Ms. Greene, eleven dollars an hour?" My eyes almost bulge out of my head, this heifer makes more than triple the amount I make a year and yet I do all of HER work! This is the first time I've realized how extremely underpaid I was. The initial remorse I felt for going behind her and Evica's back and accepting her position is now gone. I now start to slowly reconsider my initial decision.

"Separate suites in separate hotels." Hogan adds. "I've never done that in the past; usually my former secretaries die to be in the same hotel as me, let alone the same suite. For you, I will book us two separate hotels. Paparazzi can't spin a story if we're not seen together outside of the gala! Also, it's a two-night experience in a beautiful city where I'll take care of everything from your transportation to your wardrobe."

"What's the catch?" I question everything about this, it sounds way too good to be true. He wants to give me a promotion, a raise, a gown, an all-expense paid trip to DC, as well as spare my reputation... all at what cost?

"Nothing, Ms. Greene, I actually respect you. For three years you haven't so much as let me touch your shoulder. Any other woman would have been putty in my hands by now. You are a really hard worker and you deserve it more than your counterpart." I am smiling so hard my cheeks hurt, "Plus I don't want to go with Louisa and get embarrassed by her lack of intelligence." We both abruptly burst out laughing at the thought of Louisa's ghetto ass attending such a distinguished event.

"Mr. Hogan, if you're serious about the separate hotels and the raise, I would be delighted to be your guest to DC." I finally agree.

"Ahh Britney, that makes me so happy. The gala takes place early next year so for now let's keep this proposition between the both of us, at least until I have time to break the news to Evica." I nod in agreement and he smiles as he pops open the bottle of champagne that was on his desk and pours each of us a glass. "To business without pleasure." He toasts. I smile uncontrollably as I touch my glass with his.

"To business without pleasure."

Chapter 6: The Devil Wears Plaid

~2000 Present Day~

I wake up to Jeremy leaving me a goodbye kiss on my forehead.

"Good morning beautiful." He whispers as I start to slowly open my eyes. "Sorry, I didn't mean to wake you, just wanted to let you know I'm heading out." I kiss his lips, and then he begins to wear a book bag full of DJ equipment onto his back.

"Do you need help loading any speakers, Daddy?" I ask half asleep.

"No, you stay in bed. I already packed up the van." He insists.

"Okay baby, see you tomorrow evening." I yawn. He leaves out of the bedroom and I hear the front door locking from the outside of our apartment. After a few minutes I hear his company van pulling off as he voyages to a wedding gig three hours away. This is what Saturday mornings during wedding season consist of; Jeremy working eight hour days, leaving me time to misbehave. His wedding packages are typically from four- eight hours and depending on the distance of the event he sometimes is gone overnight.

I roll over in bed and check my cell phone; I have three missed calls from 'Burger Royale' boy. I saved him in my phone under that moniker and now I've grown to forget his actual name. Honestly I am done with him; he is definitely only one-night stand material. I remember weeks earlier being obsessed with his beauty, but now that I've seen Greg, I'm so over him. Greg is still the most handsome man I've ever laid eyes on; too bad messing with him would only bring drama in my life. Burger Royale boy was so blatant with his gold digging that it became a turn off. Don't get me wrong, I know what it is when I'm getting into one of these crazy sexual affairs, but I get a rush from the possibility of me and whoever it is falling madly in love and running off together into the sunset. I get a rush from playing out this fantasy, even though in actuality I have no intension of leaving Jeremy.

I decide not to call Burger Royale back and mentally put a rest to his saga. I also decide to go take a shower, put on some make-up, wear some revealing clothes, and go out in search of a new adventure/boy toy since at the moment both of my potential side-men were fails.

It is seventy degrees outside and it feels amazing, spring is creeping up on us! I am wearing short shorts that show off my thick thighs and a loose top that distastefully exposes the cleavage from my d-cup bust. My make-up is flawless and I manage to put my hair in a slick beautiful bun (which surprises me because my hair has never been so cooperative). With each step I take I get a whiff of the perfume I sprayed myself with before I left my apartment. I typically never wear perfume, but Greg inspired me to start, since every time I was around him, he smelled like heaven. Yep, I am ready for the hunt. My pussy is throbbing at the thought of flirting with some fresh meat. With Jeremy and I being so busy with conflicting work schedules, I haven't had any sex since the night I spent with Burger Royale boy, so I am extremely horny... and ready.

I end up at the Morehouse coffee shop, located roughly three blocks from my apartment complex and directly across the street from the Vacation Inn. As I sip on my white chocolate mocha, I gaze out the window at the hotel hoping I'd be spending my night there with a sexy new stranger later that evening.

"Britney?" A deep voice snaps me out of my deep thoughts. "Wow, it's been a long time." My heart stops... Standing directly in front of me is Anthony Johnson, my ex-lover AKA the man I trace my emotional issues back to.

"Hi." I let out still processing the fact that he is standing directly in front of me.

"How've you been? My God, what's it been like seven years?" His excitement is cute; he looks genuinely happy to see me even though I cursed him out via email the last time we spoke. I think the email went something like: [HOW THE FUCK ARE YOU MARRYING THIS BITCH? WE'VE ONLY BEEN BROKEN UP FOR SIX MONTHS!] He never did respond.

"Yea, it's definitely been a while." I start to blush; I *still* can't believe I am face to face with Anthony Johnson right now... And he looks damn good. At thirty years old, he is sexier than I remember, age did nothing but add to his beauty. His body looks more built than I remember and he's dressed casually in a plaid red shirt that drapes beautifully over his upper body, tugging ever so slightly at the mounds made by muscles. The only thing extremely different about him is his neatly shaped goatee; he had no facial hair back when we dated. "How've you been?" I manage to let out.

"I've been doing well, can't complain at all." He smiles as big as a car salesman, that's when I notice his gold necklace and the Rolex on his wrist. I start to wonder if he still held on to the five-hundred-dollar G-Wack watch I got him back in the day. I know they're no longer that popular but I remember him being so happy and wearing it all the time. I spent my birthday money on that watch, but by the looks of the Rolex I see he's moved on to bigger and better things. Just then the barista calls out his name and he goes and picks up his coffee. I convince myself that if he comes back to my table and sits down he wants to fuck me. I've only fraternized with one other married man in my lifetime and it ended horribly, but I am willing to try it one more time because this right here was fate. I haven't seen Anthony since he moved out of state with his wife shortly after their wedding, and now

48

he is in the same coffee shop as me on a day I am on a hunt. Sure enough, after picking up his coffee he comes right back to my table… Game on.

"So do you live around here again?" I continue the conversation as he sits down across from me. He takes the top off of his cup to reveal pitch black coffee; he empties and stirs in two sugar packets. *Black coffee? Typical… Must match his heart and soul*, I think to myself as he takes a sip.

"No. No… Tina and I still live out of state; I'm just back here visiting my mother." He smiles.

"Oh ok." I cringe when he mentions Tina, his wife. I look around the coffee shop trying to find her face among the other coffee shop patrons. I've never met her in person but I know her face from weeks of studying pictures of her on her wedding day, which I acquired from our mutual friends. I am relieved when I don't see her in the shop. I grin, what's that saying people use, 'out of sight, out of mind'?

"So what do you do? Are you married?" He asks. I am not shocked by the blunt questioning; Anthony was always nosey and materialistic. Even at twenty-three working at the mall he was all about his image, he had to have the nicest clothes, always had a haircut, and because of this he was extremely popular in our neighborhood growing up. He would always suggest outfits for me to buy and wouldn't hesitate to let me know when I could afford to lose a few pounds.

"Yea, I'm engaged…" I feel him look down at my ring finger, "Don't have a ring yet, but we live together and we're currently saving up for one."

"Oh wow, little Britney, finally tying the knot! Good for you." I am not used to this Anthony, so upbeat and grown up. Even though he was in his twenties back then, he was always really immature.

"Yep, and I work at Hogan and Wildes." I add, proud of myself, knowing he'd be envious.

"WOW, Hogan as in his son of the billionaire oil tycoon, Hogan?"

"Yep, I work at his law firm. I'm a legal secretary, and you?" I intentionally drop the *assistant* in my job title.

(Even though Hogan has made me a verbal offer, nothing is official until it's documented).

"That's what's up, make that bread mama, I am not mad at you. Me? I work for Tina's dad; he owns a lot of restaurants across the west coast. He hired me shortly after we got married; he's not 'Hogan rich' but he's definitely not too far behind." He smiles and stares deep in my eyes… I melt. Right now, I want to fuck him so bad. I'd forgotten how beautiful he looked; he's always had the fullest lips but now that he has this goatee thing going on, it accentuates his succulent lips even more. I want to reach over the table and suck on them slowly, but I refrain from acting a fool in public. He must sense what I am thinking by looking into my eyes because he quickly turns away. He knows what calling me 'mama' did to me back then, and evidently it still gets me wet to this day.

"So what are your plans for the rest of the day?" I ask with bad intentions.

"Oh I'm waiting for Tina." He says checking his Rolex. "She's at the mall and will come pick me up from here when she's done." My heart sinks. That doesn't leave me with too much time to make my move.

"So you're too good for the mall now?" I laugh trying my hardest to play off the heart ache.

"Yep… I hate malls, you know that!" He was referring to the nights we would spend on the phone, back in the day, where he'd tell me his dreams of being rich, quitting his job at the mall and moving out of Dumois. "I only shop at boutiques, or send my wife in for me."

"Well congrats on making it out, of both the mall and Dumois." I smile. "By the way you look great." I admit.

"Thanks, Mama." He smiles cheekily. There he goes again, throwing around that word that dissolves me. He knows exactly what he's doing.

"You know what calling me Mama does to me, right?" I breathe heavily biting my bottom lip staring deeply into him. I want him, enough small talk, time wasn't on my side.

"Wow… It's like that?" He smirks.

"Mhm." I nod reaching for his hand and rubbing my fingers over it lightly.

"True." He laughs "Same ol' Britney, except a little chunkier." Wait… What the fuck did he just say, *'same ol' Britney'?* And how dare he point out my weight in such a rude manner! He must sense the change in my mood because he quickly adds, "You still look good though… If your man's happy that's all that matters. And I see you still have that libido and freaky side, that's a good thing." He jokes trying to make light of the situation. Before I have a chance to curse him out, his phone rings. "Hello... Oh ok bet… I'm coming outside now." He hangs up and points outside, "Tina's here." That's when I see a silver 2000 Mercedes-Benz c280 sport (which is the newest model out) pull up in front of the shop. He gets up and begins an attempt of hugging me goodbye.

"So that's it? You don't want to meet up and hang out later?" I dodge his hug and hint at rekindling our sexual relationship.

"I mean, that's not on my mind anymore, Britney." He changes his perky mood to a more exasperated look.

"You don't miss me at all?" I ask a little emotionally wounded. Just then his wife gets out of the car and switches from the driver's to passenger's seat, and I suddenly see why he's not biting my bait. She is beautiful. The woman is glowing, and she looks like she comes from money. She is petite except for her very pregnant belly. "Wow... Congrats, I'm happy for you." I deceitfully declare.

"Thanks. This will be baby number two." He brags. "Anyways it was nice seeing you Brit." He turns to leave but I stop him, getting up behind him and grabbing his arm. I have a question, and if I don't ask it before he walks out of my life entirely, I'll go the rest of my days wondering 'why?' The man owes me an explanation, at least some sort of closure.

"Why did you marry her and not me?" I muster up the courage to abruptly ask when he turns around. This question has been the number one cause of my insecurities for the past seven years. Anthony turns to me and looks me dead in my

51

eyes before honestly responding one word that would stick with me for the rest of my life.

"Opportunity." He says so cold and dismissive. There was the answer I'd been waiting on all these years. I wasn't pretty, rich, skinny or influential enough for him. Who was I kidding, back then I didn't elevate him; he elevated me. My little gifts must have been chump change compared to the lifestyle and prominence she offered him. I finally let go of his arm after his response resonates, and he walks out of the coffee shop, and my life. I watch as he hops into the driver's seat and drives off with whatever ounce of self-esteem I had left. Fuck my life.

Chapter 7: Shallow People

~2000 Present Day~
    After Anthony drives off with his pregnant wife into the sunset, I sit a little longer with my mocha and start reminiscing about how he even entered into my life:

~1991 Flashback~
    On my eighteenth birthday, and a month before I graduated from high school, my mother had given me five hundred dollars in cash. I grew up poor so that was a big deal and the first time I had ever seen that much money at one time. I was on my way to being the first in my family with a high school diploma and my mom was so proud that she saved up that whole year to be able give me that gift. I had plans of using that money to buy a typewriter; I had never before been able to afford one growing up. I've always been interested in literature and really wanted to pursue writing, mainly journalism, and a typewriter would really help me towards achieving my dreams. I was a good girl with commendable visions for my future, and I dated an equally respectable boy named David. Despite our decrepit surroundings we both miraculously managed to stay out of trouble, we even lost our virginities to each other two years prior. The first time we had sex, it was so awkward and full of pain that we regretted every moment of the ordeal. We were both sixteen when we tried it, and we only did it because all the other couples our age kept bragging about how good it was. After David finally stuck his penis inside of me for the first time, we hated it enough to never attempt anything sexual again. It honestly felt like that two-year relationship with David only comprised of kissing, and bowling. I never felt a real flame or an intense desire for any man... until I formally met Anthony Johnson.
    So when I turned eighteen and got my birthday money from my mom, David and I had gone bowling at the Bowleria to celebrate. He was so sweet because even though I told him about my newly found wealth, he still was adamant about

paying both our entree fees. He believed in old fashioned gender roles and had too much pride to let his woman use her birthday money on a date. David was probably the only man in my entire life, other than Jeremy, that ever respected me and treated me like a lady.

I remember it was a Sunday night and the Bowleria was packed with teens and young adults. Everyone was there mingling, bowling, laughing, dancing and having fun. I remember there was one guy, whose face I vaguely recognized, posted up in the back of the bowling alley. He didn't talk to anyone but his clothes looked new and he looked a lot older than I was. All the girls were giggling and looking in his direction, he was cute but I didn't see the big deal. When David went up to bowl I tapped a girl who was sitting next to us, "Who's that guy?" I asked, "I mean I've seen him around but he never speaks to anyone. What's his story?"

"Oh that's Anthony." She blushed. "He's so sexy and older; he's like twenty-two."

"Okay..." I said, still clueless as to why girls were going crazy over him, and why he was sitting alone in the corner, not bowling, but yet all the attention was on him.

"Girl, he works at the Hugo's shoe store in the mall. He's always got the nicest Air Jordan's and his hair is always cut fresh." She boasted on his behalf, "Also he thinks bowling is for young folk and lames." She laughed.

"Then why is he here?" I mocked at his hypocrisy.

"He's Anthony Johnson; he can be wherever he wants to be." She justified in his defense. "When he went to our high school he had all the popular girls fighting over him. He just… I don't know… Has the juice." She giggled. *The juice, huh?* Her thirst for the boy piqued my interest. I had never heard anyone from my neighborhood being so mindlessly revered like a celebrity. Usually the popular kids at school were middle class and not from Dumois. They would never be caught dead in the same places us poor kids hung out. That Anthony kid was a mystery that I immediately wanted to solve. I would spend the rest of that night imagining how a girl like me could ever win the interest of a popular, stylish man like him.

Towards the end of the night I caught Anthony stepping out the back door from the corner of my eye. I lied and told David I was going to the restroom and snuck out behind Anthony. My plan was to spy on him and to learn what his interests were, and then go from there. He was leaning against the back wall of the building smoking a cigarette. I got as close to him as possible without making it seem like I had only come outside for him.

Unfortunately, my plan to be inconspicuous was a fail: "Hey." I blurted awkwardly the moment he made eye contact with me.

"What's up?" He responded with a head nod, turning back around and never again looking back in my direction.

"I'm Britney---" I began, but was interrupted when a small car pulled up beside him.

"Yo! Ant, what's good my dude?" Said a deep voice from the car.

"Everything's gravy." He smiled as he approached the hoopty and exchanged a studied multipart handshake with the deep voiced driver.

"This you?" The driver pointed at me as if I were a piece of meat.

"Nah, she's just some high school broad." He smirked speaking as if I wasn't even present... My heart sank.

"Oh ok. I heard those new G-Wack's are out bro, but they cost about five hundred dollars." The driver informed Anthony. My ears perked at the mention of five hundred dollars. Back then I swore that dollar amount was fate. I had been blessed with five hundred dollars from my mother and it would now turn into the key I would need to access Anthony's heart. I had planned on getting a typewriter for myself with the cash but at that moment, gaining Anthony's friendship and possibly more became more important to me than funding my dreams of writing professionally.

"Yea man, usually I'm the first to get shit out here but my store won't even stock those things because they know can't nobody from around here afford no G-Wack." He laughed. "You know if my store had them I would snatch a couple for us." I remember thinking, *so that's how Anthony stayed 'fresh',* he stole new shoe releases/clothing items from the store he worked at. He was the only young adult around the way to have a legit job, but he didn't make nearly enough to be as well dressed as he was. By stealing from his store he managed to always be the first in our neighborhood to have all the newest gear. I also figured out that the reason he probably didn't bowl, or buy food at gatherings was because he didn't have the money. He was a broke man making chump change at the mall perpetrating as a trendsetter, and everyone fell for it. I assumed this was the same kind of thing Evica and Louisa were doing back in the day; pretending to be trendy but really living above their means. That sort of mentality is probably what got them caught up in all that bank robbery nonsense. One would think the deception and theft would deter me from Anthony, but it did quite the opposite. I wanted to tame that bad boy, and learn from him how to have everyone eating from my hands.

The day after the Bowleria I took three buses to a middle class neighborhood where G-Wack's were sold and I bought a gold one for Anthony. I put my 'typewriter owning' dreams aside and did something for someone else in hopes of getting them to see the good in me. I then boldly took that watch to the store Anthony worked at and surprised him with my gift. He was so happy he picked me up and spun me around the store. He told me right then and there that I was his girl and kissed me on my cheek. He never asked how I got the money for it or where I got it from, all he was concerned about was that it was an authentic G-Wack and not a knock off. His popularity increased tenfold because of that watch and I was the girl that gave it to him. I broke up with David that same day and immediately became known as Anthony's girl. That was the first instance I associated spending money on a man with gaining his approval.

Don't feel too bad for my ex David, he ended up graduating and gaining a scholarship to a prestigious college out of state, while I enrolled at Dumois community college but never graduated. The rocky, one sided relationship I endured with Anthony stunted me from graduating. I spent more time with him than doing my school work and ended up flunking every class. I always wondered what my life would have been like if I had done the smart thing and gone to college with David and left shallow Anthony alone. Unfortunately, the world will never know.

Only a handful of people born and raised in Dumois have actually made it out; David, Evica, and Louisa were a few of them. Even though I live in Tooley, my apartments are still fairly close to 'old Dumois'... I think in order to really 'make it out' one would have to live in Uptown Tooley where I work, and where most of my fifth floor co-workers live. Uptown Tooley is about an hour west of the train tracks, whereas Tooley Towne Apartments are still walking distance from Dumois.

Anthony may drive a Mercedes now, but it's all thanks to his wife. I'm assuming if she ever left him so would her money. People in Dumois are so bitter about having grown up in poverty once they are exposed to the finer things in life. Anthony is like the male version of Evica. They have to wear the best looking clothes and they have to completely separate themselves from their origins in order to feel accomplished. I just hope that when Jeremy's DJ Company blows up, and if Hogan comes through with my promotion, that the two of us never become as shallow and materialistic as the others.

~2000 Present Day~

My phone rings and snaps me out of my flashback. It's Burger Royale boy; I let the call go to voicemail and take a final gulp of my mocha. Even though Anthony didn't fall for my bait I was still horny as hell. I know I said no more Burger Royale boy but I didn't feel like hunting for new meat after that dreadful encounter with my ex.

"Fuck it." I sigh and call him back despite my better judgment.

"Hello?" He answers.

"Hey."

"Hey? Girl I've been calling you for months! What, you don't fuck with your boy no more?" He complains.

"No, it's nothing like that; work has just been really busy. I'm getting a promotion."
I exaggerate.

"Oh, okay, okay. So what's up? I'm trying to relive the last time we spent together. I never had a girl treat me like that." He speaks truthfully referring to our extravagant weekend where I took him to a classy restaurant and paid for a room at the Vacation Inn.

"Oh really?" I say a little turned on that he was appreciative of a lifestyle I had introduced him to that he had never before experienced. It reminded me of the moment I had given Anthony that watch.

"Yea, really." He laughs.

"Well do you remember where the hotel we stayed in last time is?" I say in the sexiest voice I can muster up.

"Yea, of course. I could never forget." He breathes heavily.

"Well meet me there in twenty minutes." I say and then hang up. I walk to the Vacation Inn and enter the lobby; the girl at the counter is judging me with her eyes as I book my umpteenth room with her. I swear I'm always here, she must think I'm a prostitute. I don't care though; I need some good sex. I need the kind of sex only Burger Royale boy can provide me; at this moment I don't care how rude he is or how much he uses me; I need him to take away my pain. I call him and let him know the room number.

I undress and lay on the bed waiting for my guest. I just want to get straight to the point tonight. My pussy is throbbing and wet and my ego is terribly wounded. Not up to thirty minutes goes by when I hear a knock on the door of the hotel room... He's here.

Chapter 8: You Need Jesus

~2000 Present Day~

     Its six a.m. Sunday morning. I am walking down the street from the Vacation Inn, stumbling towards my apartment complex, extremely hung over and dizzy. I'm so glad nobody is outside this early because I'm embarrassed by this walk of shame. After what feels like an eternity, I finally reach my building. I throw up chunks of last night's dinner before I continue up the steps towards my apartment. I struggle with getting my keys to fit in the locks but when I finally unlock my front door and turn the knob to open it, I'm startled by the sight of Jeremy standing right inside the doorway. He's back early.

     "Where the hell have you been?" He barks at me.

     "Chill, my head hurts." I say while scurrying past him towards the bathroom, too tipsy to realize the mess I have created for myself. I usually always have an excuse prepared for when I stay the night out with other men. The last time I was at the Vacation Inn I told Jeremy I was on a work trip. Since last night's hook-up was somewhat random, I didn't take the time to think through and execute a cover up story. It also didn't help that Burger Royale boy brought two bottles of liquor with him to the hotel and I finished half of one on my own. I expected Jeremy would be back today, but not until about 5PM. I reek of alcohol and I'm still dressed in the same very revealing shorts I wore yesterday; it would take a miracle to get me out of this one.

     "Are you drunk?" He asks the obvious, "Answer me DAMMIT! Are you drunk?" I can hear it in his voice that he's more pissed off at me than he's ever been. Still ignoring him, I walk into the bathroom and lock it. At least in here I'll have some alone time to think up an escape plan. I take off all of my clothes, turn the shower on, hop in, and let the steaming hot water flow over my body. I'm praying my pores soak up every ounce of water needed to get me back to sobriety; I need my brain to function clearly right now. I hear Jeremy retreat to the bedroom but I know this conversation is far from over. Dreading the fight that is about to occur, I decide to take an extra-long time in the shower.

I wash in between my legs where I'm a little sore and tender. Last night was unreal; I learned the hard way that Burger Royale boy's actual name is Adam... Like *literally*, the *hard* way. I remember he screamed "WHAT'S MY NAME?" While on top of me, and when I didn't have an answer for him, he figured out that I didn't actually know his name and started to fuck me the hardest I've ever been penetrated my entire life. He had me in the most compromising, uncomfortable positions, knocking my head into the headboard with every exaggerated stroke. He did all this while panting, "ADAM! MY FUCKING NAME IS ADAM!" The sex was just as intense as the first time we did it, if not ten times better, but by the end of the night he went back to his obnoxious, shallow, gold digging ways, and left me in the hotel room alone. He claimed sleeping there would seem too 'relationship-like', and he wasn't comfortable with 'that kind of thing'.

BANG! BANG! BANG! Jeremy's pounding on the door shakes me out of another day dream. He sounds livid. I would be mad too if it was the other way around and he came home drunk with no answers for me. I think I'm sobering up now because I'm currently overwhelmed with fear and sadness. I'm scared that I might lose him if I don't come up with an amazing alibi, and I'm sad because I can sense that he's really hurt.

Okay brain, this is Do or Die. You have to tell him *something*, and that *something* has GOT to be good. I run through a list of people I hope would vouch for me... It's an extremely short list. Damn, this would be a great time to have female friends in my life, but since I have none, I have to think of a family member that will help me, one that always has my best interest at heart. I leave the shower on and hop out of the bathtub; drenching the entire bathroom floor. I walk towards my cell phone, and grab it off of the rim of the sink. Still a little nauseous, I manage to pull up my mother's contact information and hit the call button.

"Hello?" My mother answers the phone with a little hint of shock in her voice, most likely surprised to hear from me. We haven't spoken since the day I kicked her out of my apartment for bringing up, and scolding me for something I did a long time ago.

"Hi mom, it's me." You can hear the desperation in my voice.

"I know who this is; I'm just ever so surprised that you decided to bless me with a phone call, Queen Britney." She is being so sarcastic, any other day I would have snapped back at her with a smart/disrespectful remark, but today I needed a favor.

"Mom, look. I'm in a big mess-" I start to say.

"What else is new?" She snaps before I can even finish my thought.

"MOM, PLEASE!" I beg her.

"What is it, Britney?" She sounds a little worried now. I let out a sigh before I speak. There is no way this holier than thou woman is going to help me cover up a lie to Jeremy, but at this very moment she is my only option.

"If Jeremy calls you, can you please tell him I was with you last night?" I whisper into the phone.

"Say what now?" At this point she's back to sounding pretty pissed.

"He's really mad at me for not coming home last night and I don't want to hurt him. Can you please just tell him I was with you if he calls?" I repeat now almost begging.

"Absolutely not!" She cackles. "If you don't want people to be hurt by your actions, then DON'T HURT PEOPLE WITH YOUR ACTIONS! Damn Britney, you have not changed, nor have you learned ANYTHING. You not only look like your father, but you act just as filthy."

"What? No Mom, you got it all wrong, I was at a work event."

"Oh... Yea... *Sure* Britney. I wasn't born yesterday; you know? I know damn well you had your legs open to someone other than Jeremy last night. You sound like you're drunk!" I hear her turn away from the phone and murmur,

"Where did I go wrong, Lord Jesus, where did I go wrong?" She starts to cry.

"Ma, please stop, I did not *cheat* on Jeremy. I was out with some work friends."

"YOU'RE A DAMN LIAR!" Her volume made me jump. "YOU'RE ALWAYS LYING AND MESSING UP A GOOD THING!" Emma Greene is clearly over my antics.

"Mom, I'm going to go now, because obviously you're still harboring a lot of anger towards me over something I did more than four years ago, and like I told you the last time you were over here, I just want some peace." As I bring the phone down away from my ear and as I'm about to hit the end call button, I hear her scream:

"JESUS! CHILD YOU NEED JESUS! IF YOU DON'T CHANGE YOUR WAYS YOU'RE GOING TO DIE, JUST LIKE YOUR FATHER! LONELY, BROKEN, AND SICK!" I hang up. I don't even know why I tried. I'm going to regret ever making that call when I completely sober up. Regardless of how horrifying the conversation went with my mother, the bright side of making the call was that I finally figured out a plausible excuse.

I turn the shower off and wrap myself with a towel. I take a deep breath, unlock the bathroom door then boldly walk into the bedroom where Jeremy is laying down fretting in bed, facing the wall. "Jer." I walk close to him and sit at the foot of the bed and lovingly place my hand on his leg. "Jer, I'm sorry I didn't tell you I was going out last night. Look, I have a surprise and I really didn't want to have to tell you about it this way. I wanted to wait until it was confirmed before I broke the good news to you. I just, didn't want to get your hopes up before I knew for sure." I should be an actor because the lies are spewing out effortlessly, I even sigh on cue and everything. Jeremy sits up and faces me staring blankly into my eyes.

"I just don't know how you expect me to trust you when you start doing things like this, Britney." He speaks so low; like he's simultaneously making life changing decisions about our future in his head.

"Did you hear me, Jeremy? I said I didn't want to ruin it and tell you, but the reason I'm just now coming home, and the reason I got super drunk last night was because I was out celebrating with everyone at work."

"Celebrating?" Jeremy still looks suspicious, but his face looks a little relieved. Poor thing is clinging on to my every word, probably praying I didn't do anything to jeopardize his love and trust. I could never tell him the truth. I could never tell him I just got my back blown out by a fast food employee probably eight years younger than the both of us. No, I could never tell him about Adam or the many other men I've taken to the Vacation Inn... So I lie.

"A couple months back, Hogan called me into his office and told me he wanted to give me a promotion. Well this week it was confirmed." I see his mood change so quickly and his eyes light up. Obviously this is a lie because Hogan and I haven't spoken about my promotion or the gala recently, but I figured this would be a good time to tell Jeremy about it. I never told him about it before today because I didn't want to get his hopes up until Hogan gave me the position in writing. Right now the news acted as a perfect deflection; desperate times call for desperate measures.

"Really?" He tries to contain his excitement because he's still a little disbelieving.

"Yes. Hogan wants to make me his legal secretary."

"What about Louisa?" Though Jeremy has never met anyone at my job, he knows most of my co-workers by name because of how much I've come home and complained about them over the years.

"He's going to demote her." I smile.

"Wow. It's about damn time. I mean, you were doing all the damn work in that place." I smile even harder after hearing his outburst of support. This is the perfect cover-up because it's based on truth, *and* its good news. I pat myself on the back... Good work, Brit!

"I know, right? So anyways, a lot of my coworkers wanted to take me out and congratulate me... Well sans Louisa and Evica, because they're pretty pissed about the whole thing. So we went to one of those new bars in Tooley last night and I got so drunk this girl in accounting let me sleep at her apartment. I needed to sleep it off babe, we all did. Nobody was sober; I didn't want to get in a car for an hour and be driven by someone just as drunk as I was, and I didn't want to stumble around taking public transportation that late at night. So I crashed at her apartment which was a block away from the bar and just woke up about two hours ago. She just dropped me off in front of the building. Jeremy, please believe me. If I had her number, I'd let you call her right now to corroborate my story. If you want, when I go into work tomorrow morning I can have her call you." I hope he's eating this all up.

"Okay." Jeremy lets out a sigh of relief. "I believe you, I was just worried. I just didn't know what happened to you. The night my brother was killed my mother and I stayed up all night wondering where he was. So last night I was having horrible flashbacks when I didn't hear from you." I can see him getting emotional. "I'm also not going to lie, when I saw you in that outfit once you finally came home, I was thinking the worse. I just didn't know where you were coming from, but now I do… so I'm good. And I apologize for jumping to the wrong conclusions without waiting for your response first." (And this is the last I ever hear of this dilemma, I love how trusting Jeremy is, he's such a beautiful, secure person on the inside. I don't deserve him at all). "By the way, who were you talking to while you were in the shower?" He inquires.

"My mother." Jeremy looks confused; he knows what the situation is between Mrs. Greene and myself. He was here the last time she was at our apartment, that was the day she called me a rotten woman and I told her to get out of my apartment and never speak to me again. There is a reason why my mother and I are at such odds:

~1994 Flashback~
    A year after Anthony Johnson left with his new wife I was an emotional wreck. I was around twenty-one, my body

65

was perky, and I was a lot prettier than I am now. I turned into such a fast, young adult. I became black like my heart and started using my body, *and money,* to get what I wanted from men; attention. I was set on making others feel as horrible as Anthony had made me feel. At the time I still lived with my mother and Jeremy wasn't even in the picture for another year.

Living directly across the street from my mother's house was a married couple who were both in their early forties; Deon and Jenna Jackson. I've known them since I was five years old when they moved in directly across the street. My mother said before the Jackson's moved into that house it was occupied by the Wildes'. Inopportunely, I was too young to know or remember a 'low income housed' Evica Wildes, but I would give anything to observe her behavior back then.

Anyways, Deon Jackson was old enough to be my father, the older I got the finer he became. Before I turned twenty-one I would have never made a move on Mr. Jackson no matter how good I thought he looked, but like I said earlier, when Anthony left, he took my self-respect with him. I had so much reckless sex after I found out he got married, it was a miracle all I ever caught in my lifetime was a brief, *cured* case of chlamydia.

Deon worked overnight stocking a thrift store while his wife, Jenna, worked as a cafeteria lady in an elementary school during the day. My unemployed ass was home all day while my mother slaved eighty hour weeks washing dishes at a restaurant to bring home chump change. The point is Deon and I were always home alone until like 9PM at night when my mother got home and he left out to go to work. Sometimes I'd see him working on his truck outside and it would turn me on, but we never spoke more than two words to each other. Crazy because I remember he used to play with me all the time back when I was a child (never inappropriately). His wife used to babysit me most summers while my mother worked double shifts.

Anyways, like I was saying after Anthony broke my heart I was sneaking Jake, a neighborhood boy who was around my age, into my mother's house. I saw Mr. Jackson peering at us from across the street; he was standing in his doorway looking in our direction, so I decided to play a little game of teasing him. I started to kiss Jake passionately, fantasizing that he was Deon instead. Poor Jake never noticed we were being watched and that I was only using him as a pawn in my games. I saw Deon from the corner of my eye looking uncomfortably from his lawn as I groped Jake. I can only imagine what Mr. Jackson was thinking, something along the lines of: 'Mrs. Greene's daughter has gone wild'. I began to grip Jakes hardening dick from outside of his pants, enjoying the fact we had an audience. Jake started grabbing onto my breasts and squeezing them from outside of my shirt.

Across the street on his lawn, Mr. Jackson kept pretending to look away and not notice what was going on, but I could feel him staring. I remember hoping he wasn't just spying on me to report all this to my mother, I prayed after seeing this he would want me as bad as I've always wanted him. Only one way to find out, so I upped the ante. I took off my shirt and bra and stood at the doorway of my mother's house half naked, I boldly and seductively looked straight at Mr. Jackson letting him know with my eyes that I wished it were him on me in place of this kid. He got nervous and almost went inside, but I gave him a devilish half smile confirming this show was for him. He looked up and down the street making sure no one else was seeing all this and when he saw it was safe, he continued to look on.

The neighborhood boy was going crazy on my nipples, licking eagerly around each areola, he had gotten so hard. I wasn't too interested in what he was doing, he was just a boy, and at that moment I had a taste for a grown man. I forget what I told the boy to have him leave abruptly. I probably lied and said I was on my period and couldn't continue, because all I remember is Jake leaving and cursing me out and calling me a "faker" because I wouldn't let him get to fourth base. As he stormed away I stood there, still completely topless, not breaking eye contact with a still heavily gazing Deon. That's when I started licking my own nipples, and he finally lost it. Mr. Jackson couldn't control his desires anymore, plus I'm sure my body was more amazing than what his forty-year-old wife could ever offer him. At that moment he ignored all consequences and crossed the street so fast he was in front of my house before I could blink. When he got to me he picked me up, laid me on the floor inside of my house, and shut the door behind him.

He began taking off his clothes as he sucked on my nipples the way they were meant to be adorned, causing them to harden. *Now this was how a real man sucked nipples*, I remember thinking to myself. After he was undressed he tugged at my jeans until I took them off. He impatiently ripped off my panties and spread my legs, then proceeded to shove his grown, enormous, raw dick inside of me. Everything happened so fast, we both had an orgasm in less than ten strokes due to the built up excitement.

When we came to our senses I could see his face filled with remorse and fear. We didn't say one word to each other the entire time, from beginning to end... Not one word. He hurriedly put his clothes back on and ran out of my mother's house, looking around nervously as he crossed the street. I stayed on the floor feeling good and smirking at the power I had discovered in between my legs. I was so hot; I could make an older, married man cheat. I felt invincible.

Anyways, long story short, when my mother came home she was furious. Apparently a neighbor witnessed the whole ordeal from inside of their house. The news of Ms. Greene's fast twenty-one-year-old daughter spread quicker than the plague. My mother and Jenna, who were good friends since I was five years old, had a rough patch in their relationship after that day. I never saw Mr. Jackson after that either, he was kicked out of his house and Jenna filed for divorce. Every time I saw Mrs. Jackson after that she'd give me a death stare. Although my mother continued to let me stay with her, our relationship was forever tarnished. So imagine how thrilled I was three years later after I snagged a job at Hogan & Wildes and was able to move out with Jeremy on our own. Tooley Towne Apartments aren't that far from my old neighborhood in Dumois, but the newly built train tracks caused a big enough divide to where Mrs. Jackson and I would rarely ever cross paths.

My mother has never forgiven me; to her I went from being her virgin angel daughter, to the devil's promiscuous spawn, all in one day. Maybe Emma is right though, maybe I do need Jesus.

Chapter 9: Like a Movie

~2000 Present Day~

    I can't believe I'm sitting on a private jet on my way to Washington DC. I've never been outside of Missouri in my entire life, nor have I ever been on any type of aircraft. Hell, the two-mile relocation I made years ago from 'poverty stricken' Dumois to where I live now in Tooley was a big deal for me. This right here… is unreal! We took off about fifteen minutes ago and I've spent the entire time gawking outside of my window. This whole experience has me mesmerized; the breathtaking bird's eye view of my state is beautiful, but it also makes life back home look so miniscule in the grand scheme of things. I've always heard Evica talk about the different places she's vacationed, but I never dreamed I'd see life outside of Missouri for myself.

    "You seem to really be enjoying the view." Hogan says smiling. I nod, way too busy to even look up at him or respond. A flight attendant comes by with champagne and refills his empty glass. "Would you like some more, Ms. Greene?" He points at my own empty glass set in the armrest of my chair.

    "Oh, no thank you. I have a one drink limit for this trip." I giggle. I wasn't born yesterday; I've known this man's intentions for the past three years. I can't show him any sign of weakness for the next couple of days. It is extremely critical to remain sober at this gala if I'm going to return home blemish free, with my head held high.

"Okay, I respect that." He fades out into the background as I start daydreaming again, this time about what DC might be like.

For weeks Jeremy and I have been researching everything about DC, from the best tourist locations to the best restaurants to dine in. We've become a lot closer after our first fight which occurred a month ago, when I came home drunk. As a business owner himself, Jeremy is well aware of how prestigious it is to be given the opportunity to attend this gala; he also understands that by me going with *playboy* Bill Hogan, I will almost definitely end up in some tabloid. As a couple, for weeks, we've weighed the pros and cons of me going and decided it was a once in a lifetime opportunity, and as long as the rumors accrued were *just* rumors, we could live with the blemished reputation I would acquire. Some of the good things, or 'pros', we came up with about me going on this trip were: 1) Hogan and I are going to be staying in separate hotels, which in itself will diminish a lot of the sex scandal rumors, 2) it is an all-expense paid trip to a city I otherwise would have never been able to visit on my own, and 3) just by attending this gala I will be subjected to a room full of potential, future investors for whatever business we decide to venture into. The plan is to turn this trip into something that will benefit our relationship financially in the long run.

"Wake up Sleeping Beauty." Hogan croons, patting me on my shoulder. 'We're here." I must have fallen asleep daydreaming about what DC would be like.

"Already?" I immediately open my eyes, the sleepiness wears off quick and now I am filled with excitement again.

"Yep, you've basically been asleep for the entire two-hour flight." He laughs.

"Good, because that's the only sleep I plan on getting this entire trip." Bill laughs at my eagerness, but I am serious;

71

I don't intend to get one lick of sleep while I'm in DC. I want to experience as much as I can with my limited time here. It's Friday evening, and we are only staying here until Sunday afternoon.

Hogan gives me a credit card with a ten-thousand-dollar limit, and instructs me to use it on whatever I want, while in the city. I also didn't have to pack a bag because he assured me there would be an entire wardrobe, sized to fit me perfectly, waiting for me in my hotel room. I feel like a very important person traveling with Bill, since I boarded the jet everyone I've crossed paths with has been extra nice to me and treated me as if I was nothing short of royalty.

As we exit the airport, we are met by two sharply dressed men, each standing in front of a separate Rolls Royce. The driver in front of the first Royce is holding a sign that reads 'ATTENTION WILLIAM J. HOGAN' and the driver in front of the second vehicle is holding up a sign that reads 'ATTENTION BRITNEY GREENE'. Seeing my name in bold on a sign held in front of a car worth a little over a quarter of a million dollars is a perk of a lifestyle I could *definitely* get used to. I just have to do everything in my power to stand out positively at this gala, and network with as many people as possible. One example of an ideal situation would be me meeting the owner of a prominent radio station, who'll give Jeremy a shot at being one of their highly paid, in-house DJs... Truly possibilities of this trip are endless.

"Separate cars to take us to our separate hotels." Bill emphasizes, smiling slyly as if to say 'see I am a man of my word'. "Your car will take you to The Hay-Adams, a five-star hotel in Northwest D.C. It's not far from where the actual gala is taking place. The whole staff there is expecting you, so you don't have to worry about checking in. Your driver has your room key and there are already fifteen different dresses in there for the gala tomorrow. Pick out whichever one *or ones* you like the most. You have my cell phone number so if you have any questions or if you need anything, please don't hesitate to call me." Hogan shifts his attention to the driver holding my name; "Britney this is Fred; he will be taking you wherever you need to go for the next couple of days until we leave DC." Fred smiles at me and gives me a half wave. I feel like I'm in the movie Pretty Woman, minus the prostituting. This is already such an amazing experience and I haven't even gotten to my hotel yet.

"Where will you be staying?" I blurt out, out of curiosity.

"Not that it matters to you since you won't be joining me at my hotel suite, but I will be staying at The Jefferson." He cunningly replies as his driver holds open the back door for him. Bill slides in the Rolls Royce and winks at me as they pull off. I run to my own car and once Fred opens the door for me, I jump in head first. I love my life, what could possibly ever go wrong on this trip? The driver shuts my door unaffected by my child-like enthusiasm, I'm pretty sure he's used to every woman Hogan brings to DC acting in the same manner.

We drive for about fifteen minutes before arriving at the Hay-Adams hotel. It towers over everything else around it and I assume it's historical, based on its vintage architectural elements. Even though buildings in DC aren't as modern as the Hogan & Wildes glass exterior property, they're beautiful in their own way and they're all enormous. I've never seen anything like them in real life, I feel like I'm arriving at the Buckingham Palace on my way to visit the Queen. We don't have skyscrapers or massive monuments in my city; even my apartment complex isn't built high.

The Hay-Adams makes the Vacation Inn look tiny and decrepit. Everything from the lobby to the staff is welcoming and remarkable. Being here reminds me of the first time, three years ago, that I set foot inside of Hogan & Wildes and was in awe by its contemporary decor. It's like entering a building where everything is as meticulously hand crafted as Bill's imported office door. I can see myself in the shiny marble floors, and all the elegantly scattered mirrors and paintings make it feel as if I'm walking through a museum.

When I finally get to my suite I am at a loss for words, it has to be five times the size of my actual apartment back home. Hell, it *is* an apartment, there is no way this can be a hotel room! It is equipped with a kitchen, gym, gigantic bedroom, a dining area, and a seating area with a TV the size of Africa set in the corner of the room. I also notice four racks of clothing loaded with everything from daily wear to ball gowns. I recognize a lot of the names tagged on to the clothing as some of the top designers in the world. I swear Hogan has turned my suite into a luxurious boutique. Holding one of the gowns up against my figure, I hop on top of the California king sized bed and start jumping up and down like an adolescent; swirling for joy. Where has this all been my entire life? I suddenly notice a fresh bouquet of roses on a side table in the other room. I gently place the dress on the bed as I hop down and head towards the roses. I open up a card that is attached to the vase, and it reads:

"Looking forward to spending this weekend with you. I know we only agreed to being seen together at the gala tomorrow night, but it would be an honor if you would meet me at Marcel's restaurant for Dinner tonight at 9PM as a pre-celebration.

-Bill"

Was this man crazy? I'm not about to risk being caught alone in a restaurant with playboy William J. Hogan! I can see the paparazzi now, taking a picture of the two of us in that romantic setting and that picture blowing up and making headlines. I understand Bill has given me this lucrative opportunity, and I appreciate him for it, but dinner and roses were not a part of the deal. I ball up the card and shoot it into a trash bin about a foot away from me. Besides, I already have plans for my Friday night, it's my first night in the capital of the WORLD… and I am going to see the White House!

~The Next Day~

The night of the gala has finally arrived. Fred drops me off in front of the Cordon Rouge; which is the venue the first part of the event is being held in. As soon as he opens the car door for me, I am immediately swamped with flashing lights and camera men calling at me from all different directions. "What designer are you wearing?" They chant. "Olivier Vasquette!" I reply, not knowing I would have to repeat this same dialog over a hundred times throughout the course of the night. Olivier Vasquette is the French designer responsible for this twelve thousand dollar, flowing, earth toned garment that is stunningly draped around my figure. The dress compliments the shape of my body by allowing my cleavage to shine tastefully, and by pinching in my waist tight enough to give me a coke bottle figure. For the first time in my life my hair, makeup, and nails are all flawless. There are other women walking the same carpet more notable and acclaimed than I am, but I feel everyone's eyes spellbound on me. Nobody knows who I am or who I'm in attendance with, but they must figure since I pulled up in a 2001 Rolls Royce, and since I'm wearing a top notch designer dress, that I'm important. I finally understand what it must have been like for Cinderella, to go from being in rags her whole life to being the fairest lady at the ball.

Bill and I arrive separately at the gala; I told him I'd prefer meeting him at the actual event and he obliged. I want to avoid us being linked in the public's eye as much possible. I'm sure he's probably sick of me at this point, he's done nothing but spoil me since we've been here, but instead of meeting him for dinner last night I went sightseeing with Fred as my guide. In fact, I haven't returned any of Hogan's calls or messages since I arrived at my suite; the last time we spoke was at the airport. I've been having an awesome time alone, last night I had an amazing dinner at Old Ebbitt Grill; a highly recommended, cornerstone restaurant located right by the White House. After I ate, Fred even drove me past some museums. Unfortunately, almost everything was closed so I ended up just going to a random club and partying until 4am… hence my time in this beautiful city hasn't been misused. Today I spent all morning getting my hair, nails, and makeup professionally done so I didn't have time to further explore the city. Tomorrow our flight leaves at noon so I doubt I'll be able to experience anything other than this gala, but I vow to return here with Jeremy one day and really just fully enjoy the city.

When I finally enter the venue I am shocked by the striking set up with over twenty beautifully set dinner tables placed strategically around an enormous, magnificently lit stage. It looks as elegant as some of the award ceremonies I have seen on TV. I am led by the venues staff, all the way to a table directly in front of the stage where a very handsome William Hogan stands at the sight of me and pulls out my chair. *Wow*, he looks amazing in his black tuxedo. His hair is perfectly slicked back and the part in it must have been created by God Himself. Seeing how well he cleaned up has me feeling nervous and insecure. I start to feel like I don't belong here. I know the company I work for is one of the corporations being honored at this gala, but I didn't think we'd be seated VIP style, centered directly in front of the main stage. Hogan deserves all these accolades; he single-handedly led a law firm into one of the top businesses in the entire country, whereas I on the other hand, am just a legal secretary's assistant.

"It's nice of you to show up and bless me with your presence, Ms. Greene." Bill whispers into my ear as we both get settled into our seats. There are six other couples at our table, all looking just as rich and successful as Hogan. The names of each company they represent are set in front of them inscribed into a gold block. That's when I notice the one directly in front of Bill and me. I reach out and flip it over to see Hogan & Wildes, LLP beautifully carved into it. I wonder how much this solid block of gold is worth, it is extremely heavy, I even contemplate putting it in my purse and taking it back to Missouri with me. That's when I feel Hogan nudge me underneath the table, I assume it's his way of telling me to 'put the damn thing down and focus on what is starting up on stage'.

The lights dim in the venue and a live orchestra begins to play behind the stage as an announcer proclaims, "WELCOME, LADIES AND GENTLEMEN, TO THE FOURTEENTH ANNUAL BUSINESS GALA IN WASHINGTON DC." Just then a waitress walks by to fill the champagne glasses of everyone at my table and I immediately raise mine, fuck all that 'sober' shit I was talking about on the jet, I need a damn drink!

After periods of fake smiling, fake laughing, and faking feeling like I belonged, the presentation portion of the gala came to an end. Bill is called to the stage to accept the excellence award for his law firm and its sustained success and growth for the past six years. When he speaks the room is silent, I am in awe at how engaging his personality is and how comfortable he looks on stage. There is definitely a power in his presence, I glance across the room at all the attention he's commanding as he speaks so eloquently; he is so charming. After he's finished his speech is received with a standing ovation as he makes his way back to our table. I stand up and join the applause, realizing *just now* that William J. Hogan is a great man.

It is now 11PM and the formal portion of the gala is over, it was the longest three hours of my life and took a downward spiral after Hogan spoke. I am relieved to be able to go back to my hotel suite and change into something more comfortable for part two of the gala; *the after party*. This is where more drinks are poured and people really have the chance to mingle and network. My goal is to focus on owners of publishing houses (because deep down I still have a dream of being an author one day), and radio station owners; for Jeremy.

At my suite I pick out a sexier, less strenuous dress designed by Louie Verdone. It is red, flows loosely around my midsection, and is cleverly designed to cover all my problem areas. I must say, I look extremely sexy for no longer wearing a corset. I choose this dress to be able to move freely on the dance floor, because thanks to all the glasses of champagne I had during part one of this gala; I am now ready to cut loose. I pair the short red dress with some shiny black, red bottom heels, and some vibrant, red lipstick... I am ready to knock 'em dead!

This time Fred drops me off at the Bell Dome, which is where the meet-and-greet portion of the event is being held. It is just as spectacular as everything I've seen so far, and Fred tells me there is a big fairytale-like ballroom on the inside. Hogan and I meet at the entrance and walk in together. He looks just as amazing as he did earlier except we unintentionally coordinated this time, him wearing a red shirt inside his suit. He smiles when he sees me. "You look absolutely beautiful, Britney." Hogan speaks while getting extremely close, and I can feel his bottom lip brush up against my earlobe. The contact sends shockwaves throughout my body. Uh, oh... I was suddenly becoming very weak.

I knew I shouldn't have been drinking all that alcohol earlier. I'm not drunk but I'm a little too free spirited at the moment to be hanging around my sexy, married, ill-intentioned boss. Just when I think I am going to melt where I stand, Bill places his hand on my lower back and walks me inside the ballroom; more shockwaves, and this time I feel wetness in my panties.

The night is full of dancing and flirting. I successfully complete the mission by attaining the business cards of over twenty people I feel could really help advance Jeremy and me in the fields we're interested in. I've been saying all the right

78

things, being very engaging, and just really showcasing my personality. The liquor brings out a witty side of me I never even knew I had.

The time is now 3AM Sunday, and everybody is leaving out to go back to their respective hotel establishments. I have just settled into the back seat of my Rolls Royce and Fred is literally just about to pull off when I hear a loud slamming coming from the side of the car.

"What the fuck?" I react, a little frightened thinking we might have hit someone. I roll down my window and see a tipsy William J. Hogan is cheekily staring me down. I sigh, "What do you want Hogan?" I pretend to be annoyed when secretly my heart jumps.

"I need a ride to my hotel. My driver isn't here yet and I'm not trying to sit out here waiting for him." He smiles as he lets himself into the car. This man thinks he's slick. How the hell would his driver drop him off but forget to pick him up? As well trained and professional as Fred is; I highly doubt Hogan's driver is any less punctual.

"Whatever Bill, just get in and keep your hands to yourself… And don't try anything funny." I say jokingly, even though I'm extremely serious. This whole night together has put us in a more comfortable, friend-zone type of relationship.

"Yes, ma'am." He says playfully as he lays out in the back seat and slyly places his leg on my lap. "I'm just glad you finally called me Bill." He smiles and I can't help but smile back. After hanging out with Bill all day I realize he's not that bad of a person, I'm actually feeling extreme gratitude towards this man. He falls asleep on the way to his hotel and I end up staring at him the entire time… He really is extremely beautiful.

"We're here!" Fred exclaims as he pulls into the beautifully lit entrance of The Jefferson. Hogan sits up and is ready to exit the car when he catches me ogling the establishment.

"Did you want to see the inside?" He asks, knowing I am easily impressed since I come from a small shit town in Missouri. He is probably reminded of the first time I interviewed for a job at his company and how mesmerized I was by the modernly constructed building.

"I don't know…" I reply hesitantly.

"Oh come on! Just really quick, Fred will be right here waiting on you." He insists.

"Okay," I say giving in. "Just a quick look." He is elated as he helps me out of the car. When I walk into the building I look like a little kid in a candy store. "This is so, so, so beautiful." I say as I immediately get ready to turn back around and go back outside to meet Fred.

"Don't you want to see my suite, Britney? I promise you it only gets better."

"I really don't think that's a good idea." I contest with every ounce of fight I have left in me.

"I know your suite is beautiful and all, because I've stayed there before, but I guarantee you it is NOTHING compared to mine." He brags, "Trust me! You're not going to want to miss seeing this."

"Okay." I agree, giving in again.

Bill swipes an electronic key and the double door entrance to his suite automatically swings open revealing heaven on earth. At first sight, without actually stepping foot inside the room I can see a basketball hoop, a Jacuzzi, and some exotic plant life. "Wow." I say under my breath. Hogan takes my hand and drags me deeper into his den. It is so big it feels like it occupies the whole floor as oppose to being one of many rooms on said floor. He drags me all the way to the seating area right next to his enormous bed.

"Would you like a drink mademoiselle?" He asks playfully.

"No thanks, I've had enough already." I chuckle nervously. "I actually think I should get going, I don't want to be rude and have Fred waiting out there too long." As I get up to leave, Bill chases me to the door and stands directly in front of me, blocking my way.

"Britney... Fred is gone."

"What?" I ask annoyed. I knew this whole thing was a set up. "I want to leave NOW!" I yell, at this point I am extremely furious.

"Britney, calm down." He grabs my waist and attempts to pull me into him. "I just want to talk to you." He begs as I push him away.

"GET THE FUCK OFF ME! Like what the FUCK Hogan? Do I not make myself clear at work? I've been turning you down for the past three years... IF I WANTED TO FUCK YOU I WOULD HAVE ALREADY FUCKED YOU!" I blurt out letting my anger get the best of me. He falls to his knees and starts hugging me at my hips. I can feel his arms on my skin underneath my already short dress.

"Britney please, just listen to me. I don't know why, but you drive me crazy! All I'm asking for is one night with you. I swear nobody will know about this. We've taken all precautions to not be seen in tabloids, please just let me make love to you." He cries. He then places his hands around my ass and begins hungrily groping me. I am only wearing a thong underneath the thin dress, so he is able to fully grip my bare ass. I start to get a little turned on by his actions but I still fight the urges.

"Bill you can have anyone you want! Why do you insist on ruining me?" I bark, pretending to be unfazed.

"I want to do the opposite of ruin you, baby girl! I brought you here; I gave you this opportunity... and guess what? I know we've briefly talked about it once, but after how well you did tonight, I want to officially give you the legal secretary position." I freeze at his words. Is this really happening? He hasn't brought up my promotion since that one time in his office last year, am I really about to be making eighty-five thousand dollars a year? I am close to tears.

"Please don't play with me." I say crying from tears of joy. Hogan gets back on his feet and begins kissing my neck.

"Baby, I'm not playing with you, please trust me. I want you so bad, and I want to give you the job. That's why I asked you to dinner Friday night... I was going to tell you all this then." He continues while passionately sucking on my neck.

"Show me the paperwork first." I still didn't fully trust him, and if I am going to go against my morals and give him the goods, I need everything he ever promised me in writing. Hogan takes his lips off of my neck, stomps towards his closet, grabs his briefcase, and throws a manila folder at my feet. I pick it up and take a few minutes skimming through exactly what he had verbally offered me. It is a contract/job description, and I love everything about what I'm reading. I come to the end of the document which is signed by him and only missing my signature. "Give me a pen." I demand. He impatiently reaches in his briefcase and hastily throws me a pen. I catch it and sign all the paperwork. Before I even get a chance to dot the 'I' in my name, Hogan sweeps me off of my feet and places me on his enormous bed. He rips the straps off of my expensive red dress and exposes my red lace sequenced bra. He immediately rips my bra off too, along with my red thong. I guess making him wait for three years has brought out this animalistic behavior in him.

At this point I completely give in and I want him as bad as he wants me. I tug at his belt until he begins to undress completely. Once his hardened manhood is free, I playfully shove him on his back and begin to kiss from his chest to his groin. When I get to his dick I deep throat it, ignoring my reflexes and taking it as far into my throat as possible. I am lost in his taste and the adrenaline of the moment. Hogan is pleasantly surprised at my skills and grows even harder within the depths of my mouth. He suddenly flips me around on top of him so that my legs are clenched around his head and his penis is still penetrating my mouth. We start to hungrily taste each other until we both are extremely close to climaxing. Just when I am about to cum, Bill turns me over on my stomach and forces me onto my knees. He perks my ass up, and buries my face deep inside a pillow. I can't see anything, but I can hear him wrestling with a condom wrapper behind me. I'm expecting to feel something hard thrust deep inside of me; instead I feel more of his soft, wet tongue at the entrance of my vagina. Hogan continues eating my pussy from the back like an animal, and it feels so damn good I explode with pleasure.

"Oh my God, woman you taste so good." He croons while his tongue stays busy licking up all of my cream. "I've wanted to do this for three years." He says breathing heavily. "Now let me get mine." He smiles while simultaneously kneeling up, pushing his hard dick inside of me. Bill begins to stroke me like he'd been waiting an eternity for my pussy. He pounds the shit out of my already sensitive and throbbing vagina until I go numb. I keep cumming over and over again every couple of minutes. This was my first time experiencing an hour long, multiple orgasm. It feels like never-ending pleasure and pain every time he pushes into me and my fat ass smacks into his groin area. Just when I think I can't take another stroke, Hogan quickly pulls out of me, removes the condom from around his dick, and loudly finishes all over my ass. We both immediately fall into the bed and pass out, jointly making some of the best porno movies look like child's play.

Chapter 10: The Backlash

~2000 Present Day~

    It is extremely hard returning to work on Monday morning. I've been in somewhat of a trance all day. Since coming back home from my DC trip yesterday, I've felt disgusted in myself. I basically traded sex for workplace advancement, which is something I vowed I would never do. To me, my actions were parallel to those of a prostitute's. Every other time I have had sex with a man it has been for pleasure, never personal gain; this was an all-time low for me. I also had a hard time looking Jeremy in the eye when he picked me up from the airport last night. I didn't share any real details of my trip with him, due to guilt; I just pretended to be exhausted and went straight to bed.

    One of the only positive things that came from accompanying Hogan at that gala is my new wardrobe. With my ten-thousand-dollar allowance I purchased new clothes for both Jeremy and I, Jeremy was perplexed by how I left with zero luggage but came home with ten "filled to capacity" suitcases.

    This morning when I arrive at work, I feel so uneasy. I don't know what possessed me to wear this dark blue, tailored skirt suit on my first day back, knowing damn well everyone at work will be judging me for it. Once I conjure up the nerve to actually walk into the building lobby, the first person I see as the elevator doors open up is Jane from accounting. By the direction the elevator arrived, I can tell she was coming from the basement, probably just finished philandering with Greg. I wonder how close they've become since I've taken myself out of the equation. I still haven't spoken to Greg since the day he dropped me off at my apartments months ago.

    "Good morning, Britney." She utters malevolently, putting unnecessary emphasis on my name.

    "Hi." I let out abruptly attempting to avoid any further conversation.

    "Nice outfit," She eggs on. "What is that, the Louie Verdone spring collection?" She scoffs.

"Yea, I guess." I say trying my best to downplay the refinement of my fifteen-hundred-dollar suit.

"Must have been a *great* trip." She smirks as the elevator doors open up on her floor. I haven't stepped foot on the third floor since the day I gave those accounting bitches a piece of my mind. As soon as Jane gets off the elevator I aggressively push on the door close button, the last thing I want is to be in the same elevator with another fake broad asking me about my new suit. I've never regretted wearing an outfit more than I do today. I should have waited weeks until rumors surrounding my trip to DC subside before shoving any new shit in people's faces. I say a prayer when the elevator is passing the fourth floor; I pray that God will get me through this work day without me being humiliated or disrespected at the hands of my fake ass co-workers.

Once the elevator doors open up on the fifth floor, the first person I see is an unusually gloomy Evica Wildes. She doesn't even pretend to tolerate me and say good morning. I know she never really liked me from the beginning, but she would always at least put up a front and sing good morning as she walked by me. Today, she doesn't even look in my direction.

"Okay?" I say under my breath as I watch her stomp away ignoring my existence. I wonder what the fuck Hogan has been spreading around the office. We haven't spoken since we had sex early Sunday morning in DC. That morning after the whole ordeal, I waited until Bill fell asleep then beckoned Fred to drive me back to my own hotel. Even the Jet ride on the way back to Missouri was quiet and awkward. Bill made sure to be on a two-hour business call the entire flight. He avoided making direct eye contact with me and it made me feel even more stupid and used. When we landed in Missouri we both went our separate ways. I swear to goodness, the documents I signed in DC better be honored since I'm going through all this petty bullshit. I feel my phone vibrate right before I get to my desk. It's a missed call from my mother; I also see that she's left me a voicemail:

*"Hey Britney, I know we haven't spoken for like a month since you called me drunk, but you're still my daughter and I have a right to be concerned about you. There is a tabloid in the grocery store with a picture of you and your boss at a gala in DC? You guys are dancing awfully close, and the headline reads 'Hogan's New Toy!' I just want to make sure this headline is a lie and you're not over there messing with another married man, especially your boss. Please Lord Jesus, let this be a lie. Do you think about anyone but yourself? What about his wife? What about Jeremy, why do you keep making-- *Message Deleted*"*

I can't take anymore of her nagging, so I delete the message before it even finishes playing. I don't feel the need to justify my actions, especially when my mother already has a permanently negative, preconceived perception of me. Every woman to ever go to DC with Hogan had their reputation smeared, I had already prepared for this. Jeremy already knew something like this would happen, so I know he isn't going to be mad seeing the tabloids. Hell, if anything I deserve props from him for bringing him back all those radio executive contacts that I know will really help further his career. Plus, as far as Jeremy knows, nothing even happened between Bill and me on the trip and the tabloids are full of

86

lies. When I finally get to my desk, Louisa doesn't even bother looking up at me.

"Good morning." I say anyways, trying not to let the tomfoolery of others bring me down.

"Walk of shame?" She begins to laugh, referring to my slow stroll to my desk.

"What's that supposed to mean?" I snap back with an attitude.

"Nothing, just looks like you're ashamed of something." She pokes.

"No Louisa, I'm just exhausted from the whole trip." I roll my eyes attempting to play off any suspicion.

"*Right*." She chuckles, "You sure you're not exhausted from all that fucking you did?" That is the straw the breaks the camel's back, I jump out of my seat and I'm on my way to strangle Louisa, when Evica suddenly appears in between us.

"What the hell are you doing?" Evica expectorates.

"Nothing." I retreat, regaining self-control in an attempt to keep my job. I can't let them see the tears building up in my eyes so I storm in the direction of Bill's office in hopes of getting some reinforcement. When I knock on his door I hear some scuffling before a red head I recognized from the HR department scurries out. "I swear every time I knock on your office door it's like I just switched the light on in a kitchen in the projects; roaches start scurrying everywhere!" I express half-jokingly, half jealous, but Bill isn't amused.

"How can I help you, Britney?" He asks while adjusting his tie.

"You can help me by taking care of all the slick ass comments coming from your rude ass staff." I say pointing outside of his door. At this point I can no longer control it anymore and tears begin streaming down my face. "Why is everyone, including you, treating me like shit? What the fuck did I do wrong?" I cry.

"Calm down." Hogan gets up to close and then lock his office door, "Have a seat Ms. Greene."

"No, I want to stand up." I get extremely stubborn when I feel hurt. "Why the fuck does everyone have something smart to say? You should tell them to back the fuck off!" I whine.

"C'mon, reprimanding staff in your defense will only further fuel the rumors… You know that! Besides they're probably just jealous of you… I mean, you do have on a top designer suit and you *were* chosen out of everyone to go to DC." He explains matter-of-factly.

"I KNOW! But damn! Nobody is even making eye contact with me; my mother called saying she saw me in a tabloid, people are being smart mouthed… Even you barely looked at me when I came into your office, you didn't even speak to me on the jet ride home! I can only take so much negativity and rejection." I rant.

"Oh Britney, I was working with HR just now and I had an important conference call on our flight back. No one is ignoring you; I thought you of all people would be stronger than this."

"Working, huh? Well you've been *working* hard as shit on everything else since you finally *fucked* me Sunday morning." I whisper. "I come in here to speak to you, and get some words of encouragement to get me through the circulating rumors, but instead I find you *working* on a new employee. Before we did anything you had all the time in the world for me, now that you've finally gotten what you've wanted, I guess it's all work and no play now, huh?"

"LOOK, WOMAN!" Hogan gets the most serious I have ever seen him, he grabs my arm and gives it a firm shake before he continues. "We both benefited form that trip. Yes, I got what I wanted, but so did you. We're even! You already knew how everyone would treat you when we got back. Fuck a reputation; you're getting a fucking promotion in a week that will allow you to make more than almost everyone out there talking shit! I gave you the opportunity of a lifetime; do you know how many of the women in Missouri wish they were you right now? Please get out of my office with this bullshit, I picked you because I thought you were a hard worker with thick skin, please don't prove me wrong." After he releases my arm I give him a hard shove before storming out of his office. I angrily walk past Louisa's desk towards the elevator

"Where you going?" Louisa calls after me.

"I'M ON LUNCH!" I bark back even though it's not even 10AM yet. I am speed walking in an attempt to hide my puffy face from her. I think she hears the fury in my tone because she decides not to pick a fight and just lets me go. I don't hear anything else from her as I board the elevator and make my way down to the lobby. I storm out of the building and find a corner away from potential spectators and begin balling my eyes out. I flash back to a time when I was young, before boys, before drama... when I was happy. Back when all I did was play all day and write stories. If only I could turn back time.

"You okay?" I am startled by a hand on my shoulder, turning around I see Greg smiling at me.

"Greg, don't look at me, I'm a mess right now." I begin to cry even harder, it was just my luck being seen at my weakest by Jane's boy toy.

"Well I was walking back inside from grabbing something out of my car when I saw you run over here... What's wrong?" He pulls me into him. His strong arms wrap around me. I immediately pull back from him. "Do I stink or something?" He jokes in a failed attempt to get me to smile.

"No, it's just with all the fucking drama surrounding my trip with Hogan I don't want to be in the middle of anymore scandals." I honestly divulge.

"Yea... I'm not even going to lie; people have been talking about you and Hogan since Friday, before you left." I feel a knot in my stomach and begin crying harder. "Britney, let them talk, who cares?"

"I care." I pathetically let out as regret and pain engulf me. Maybe it is the genuine sympathy I see across his face, or the need to free my conscience, but I decide at that moment to be completely honest with Greg. "It's all true." I confess.

"What's true?" He asks.

"Me fucking Bill," I look down at the sidewalk. "I didn't go with the intentions of being a slut; I really just went on the trip for the opportunity. It just happened... We stayed in separate hotel rooms and had separate drivers! He is so conniving... and I am so fucking stupid!" At this point I'm whaling. Greg pulls me into him despite my reluctance.

"Stop girl, stop." He squeezes me harder in his arms. "You think I don't know what kind of man Hogan is?" He's speaking low now so no one can hear him. "The man doesn't even speak to me when I say hi to him because I'm in the mail room. I don't put any of what you're telling me past him. I know you're a good girl; you've just been through a lot. You got to be strong though, there's always sunshine after the storm."

"I don't know what to do? I'm all over tabloids, everyone's talking... If it didn't happen it wouldn't hurt as bad, but it's hard to brush off the pain coming from being bashed when what people are saying is actually true." I explain.

"I know... I know." He pats the back of my head while I'm nestled deep in his arms. He smells so good, my mind wanders to the first time we met by the vending machines when I first smelled his cologne. "Britney, we all make mistakes. Now learn and grow. Failure is not final; having courage to continue is what counts." In this moment, all the feelings I once had for Greg (before the drama with Jane) come flooding back. Greg is the only man besides Jeremy that treats me how I want to be treated. Without judging me, he helps me by providing the exact words of encouragement I need, and walks me back into the building. I am now ready to hold my head up high, walk back into work, and take whatever bullshit comes my way. After all, I *am* the new legal secretary for Hogan & Wildes, LLP.

Chapter 11: Opportunity

~2000 Present Day~

      It's been months since the infamous DC trip, and I honestly can't complain about a damn thing. With no college degree, I am now officially the direct legal secretary to one of the most prevalent lawyers in North America. One of the unbelievable conditions of the contract I signed with Hogan was that I was given an entire year's salary up front. Thanks to my advance, I am now cruising through the newly paved streets of Tooley in a brand new, white, S-Class Mercedes Benz, rocking my new Versace sunglasses. I feel a deep connection to this city because it reminds me of myself, and like myself, it is undergoing an extreme makeover. What was once hopeless and decrepit is now slowly blossoming into something beautiful and functional. Not only are potholes being repaired, but our public school systems are being reevaluated (which is a direct correlation to why neighborhoods have been a lot safer lately). Also construction sites for franchise establishments are popping up everywhere; proof that Tooley is on its way to becoming a captivating city.

      In the same way, a lot of changes are being made in my own personal life; Jeremy and I are stronger and happier than ever, *and…* We're currently house shopping. That's right; the little girl that grew up in the "low income housing" area of Dumois is now looking into buying her first home in uptown Tooley. After experiencing DC, I initially wanted to move outside of Missouri, but the job providing me with my amiable income is located here, and so is the demand for Jeremy's DJ services. Relocating us to a different state wouldn't make any sense for either of us at this time, plus there's a little bit of pride in buying a house close to where I was raised. With the rest of my advance, I was able to buy my fiancé some upgraded equipment which has helped further develop his business, also even though my mother and I are still at odds; I surprised her by sending her five thousand dollars which has helped with diminishing tension. No matter what the two of us are going through she will always be my mother and I love her dearly. My plan is to save enough money to one day be able to move her out of Dumois and into a house of her own in Tooley. I'm not "William Hogan" rich or anything, but just to put things in perspective; I've made more money in the past two months than I would normally make in an entire year with my old salary.

As I'm sitting in my Benz, driving home from work on this beautiful Friday night, I stumble across a Christian station and begin singing along to some praises. I start thanking God for how He's slowly changing my life for the better. This lasts for about ten minutes before my mind starts to wander off track. I suddenly start to think about Anthony Johnson. I don't know how or why my mind goes from "*thank you Jesus*" to "*if only Anthony's materialistic ass could see me now*" ... But it does.

I pull into a gas station to fill up my tank, when I notice another Mercedes at a pump adjacent to the one I'm parked in front of. It is a silver C-280 sport and it looks *extremely* familiar but for the life of me, I can't remember who I know that owns one. That's when something miraculous happens, as I'm walking inside to pay for my gas, no one other than Anthony Johnson *himself* is walking out from the mart towards his car. THAT'S WHERE I'VE SEEN

THAT CAR BEFORE! THAT IS ANTHONY'S CAR! I freeze in my tracks; *did I just think this man into existence?*

"Britney?" He looks at me obviously just as shocked as I am.

"Hey Anthony." I smile.

"Wow, I swear we just randomly keep bumping into each other." He laughs awkwardly.

"Yea... I know. Are you back visiting your mother already?" I inquire while removing my Versace shades, revealing the results of a flawless make-up routine.

"No... Well, yea... Kind of... Tina gave birth months ago. We're in town introducing Anthony Jr. to the family." He stutters.

"Oh... Well congrats!" I attempt to sound excited for him. I don't know how I just dreamed this man up, but this is weird. I was just wishing I'd see him again to show off my new and improved living conditions, and just like that, he suddenly appears at a random gas station on my way home from work! I begin to wonder if I have superpowers, I honestly never intended on seeing Mr. Johnson's discourteous ass ever again, especially since last time I saw him he left me emotionally damaged in a coffee shop.

"Yea. You look amazing, way different than the last time I saw you." He adds. I wonder what *change* in me he notices: The lighter colored straight hair? The weight loss? The twelve-hundred-dollar skirt suit? The professionally manicured fingernails? The makeup? The Versace shades? The shiny new jewelry... Or, maybe it's the car? Yea, it's definitely got to be the Mercedes; after all, it *is* a newer model than his.

"Yea, a lot has happened since you and I last spoke." I smirk.

"No kidding." He takes a fourth and fifth glance at my car before cutting to the chase and asking me what was really on his mind, "Is that yours?"

"Yep." I boast.

"Wow, *nice*... Hey do you want to go to the same coffee shop we were at last time and catch up? I got like an hour before I have to be in the house." He suggests. "My mom's making dinner and it's been a while since I've had a home cooked meal."

"HA! Yea I'll go… why not?" I agree while my conscience is doing back flips. I am finally getting the chance to brag to the world's biggest opportunist about all the grand things going on in my life.

"Ok cool, meet you there." He smiles as he walks to his car. I proceed to pay for, and fill up my gas tank, before finally getting back into my own car. I use my vanity mirror to touch up my lipstick, and run my fingers through my hair adjusting any loose strands. I'm ready.

After a five-minute drive, I walk into Morehouse Coffee Shop with what feels like a swarm of thousands of wild butterflies flying crazily in the depths of my gut. I spot Anthony already seated at the same table we were at last time we were here. I wonder if he remembers that we sat there or is it just a coincidence that he chose the same table. Everything about this day just feels so perfectly aligned and written.

"It's about time." He laughs as I sit down directly across from him.

"Shut up, Anthony, I'm here now aren't I?" I blush.

"Yes, yes you are." He says while slightly biting his lip. Memories of the two of us having sex over seven years ago flash in and out of my mind. I remember he would always bite his luscious lips in the same manner whenever I'd give him head. "Um… I ordered a black cup of Joe for myself, wasn't sure what you drank so I didn't get anything for you."

"It's ok, I'm just here to talk, don't really need any more coffee, and I had a lot of caffeine at work today."

"Work, huh? You still at Hogan's firm?" He probes.

"Yea, approaching my fourth year with them. Plus, I just got a HUGE promotion that I'm extremely thankful for."

"Oh really now?" He's clearly intrigued, "Congratulations".

"Yea it has really helped me out a lot. Now my fiancé and I can finally afford to buy a house in uptown Tooley." I disclose.

"Wow, uptown? I checked out the houses there and everything is expensive. That must mean you're making a pretty good living. I still can't believe it used to be a part of Dumois. You remember this coffee house used to be an abandoned building like twelve years ago?"

"Yea, all the homeless people used to sleep in here, and at night gangs would sell drugs out of it." I reminisce.

"Yea... Dang, we really came a long way, as a city and just the both of us. You are going to buy a house, and I moved to Cali..." He sang.

"Oh that's where you're living now?" I ask, not even hiding my amazement. "I would love to one-day visit California."

"Yea, BEAUTIFUL weather, we bought a big house out there, worth close to a million."

"That sounds amazing." I genuinely express. "I went to DC months ago and it was beautiful. It's like this area is ten years behind everywhere else. I'm just glad we're finally starting to look developed."

"Oh you were in DC?"

"Yea... with my boss, Hogan. Our firm was honored at the Annual Business Gala. I saw the White House and everything!"

"Wait." Anthony speaks abruptly. "That was you in the tabloids with Hogan?" He nearly chokes on his coffee.

"Yea." I look away, a little embarrassed.

"Man, you were the talk of Tooley! I swear even my mama briefly mentioned it when I called her months ago. I just never saw the tabloid pictures for myself, and I never in a million years would have imagined you were the 'sexy unknown guest' everyone was gossiping about."

"Well it was me... Hogan chose me out of everyone. It was an amazing experience; I was given a ten-thousand-dollar spending limit, my own suite, and I got to ride around in a Rolls Royce. It was truly a fairytale." I coo.

"Sounds remarkable."

"It was life changing."

"I see." He says motioning in the direction of my parked Mercedes.

"And that's only the beginning," I continue. "I was able to network with some amazing people and next week my fiancé is going to an interview with TXA Radio, and if he gets the job that's another large sum added to our growing income."

"Oh, he's a DJ?"

"Yea" I smile, "the best one in Tooley. He probably did your wedding. He's been doing his thing for years now. It's a legitimate LLC too." I add.

"Oh, that's what's up. We didn't have a DJ at our wedding though, we had a live band."

"Oh ok."

This is when the conversation desiccated. Was Anthony Johnson jealous? We sat in silence for five minutes while he finished off his black coffee. That shit must be just as bitter as the dark soul that resides on the inside of his beautiful body.

"Why are you so quiet?" I finally break the silence.

"Well things aren't going as good for me as they are for you." He bravely admits. "The restaurant business is hard work and Tina's dad is riding my ass about every little thing. It was a mistake to go into this with her dad. I've never worked this hard in my life, so much pressure to be perfect and it's all weighing on me. That's why I come back to Tooley so often. I miss when times were simple. I miss being 'the man' around town. It's easier for piece of gold to shine in a room full of garbage than it is for it to shine in the midst of more gold."

"What?" I ask confused.

"A piece of gold; which is what I was living in Dumois back in the day, I was like a freaking king in this area, now living around a whole rack of equally successful people, I go unnoticed. I'm just a country boy to them rich folks." He elaborates. Did this piece of shit just call me garbage? Is that all this town is to him? Is that how he sees himself in comparison to the rest of us? He must have seen the disgusted look on my face because he quickly said, "Not you of course. You're not garbage. You've done so much more than a lot of the other broads around here and you didn't even have to marry rich like I did." He laughs nervously at his back handed compliment.

"Yea well, I am doing a lot with my life, thank you for noticing. And when I get a little more money saved up I'll be moving my mother out of Dumois too." I wasn't going to let this man talk down about me or my city. He was just another lost Evica Wildes. I will never forget where I came from and talk down on my humble beginnings.

"What about us?" He blurts out catching me off guard. I choke a little bit before responding.

"What do you mean what about us? What about *us*?" Anthony reaches for my hand the same way I had reached for his months earlier, while sitting in the same exact spot, at the same exact table, in this same exact coffee shop. At this point I am CONVINCED I am a witch that controls my surroundings.

"I don't know why I thought I was over you, but I'm not. I want you, Britney." He confesses. I move my hand from underneath his.

"Anthony, I'm engaged. And you're married." I remind him.

"I know, but you always were amazing at giving head." He honestly reveals. He never told me this before. "You're the only girl that has ever made me cum just off giving me head." He continues. "My wife doesn't even suck my dick."

"Oh well I'm sorry to hear that." Now I have a hard time looking him in the eye. This was so out of character for Anthony to beg, the whole time I've ever known him I was always the aggressor when it came to anything sexual.

"There's a hotel right there, you want to get a room?" He smiles cheekily, pointing at the Vacation Inn which was directly across the street.

"Like I said, I don't think that's a good idea. Don't you have to be somewhere in like ten minutes?" I am still dazed at the irony of our role reversals.

"What, dinner? My mom may still live in Dumois but we have a microwave, Britney. I can reheat that shit." He attempts to take another jab at our old neighborhood. As if having a microwave is something extraordinary that doesn't come standard in government housing. Brand-New-Anthony really got on my nerves.

"Well I can't, I'm sorry."

"Don't act like you don't cheat on your fiancé Britney, I'm hip to the new you." He attacks.

"EXCUSE ME?" I ask, waiting for him to clarify his rude statement.

"I met you when you were a good girl, but now you're basic. You were all over tabloids for being a fucking unprincipled mistress months ago, now all of a sudden you're holier than thou?" He scoffs.

"First of all FUCK BOY! I never fucking denied cheating on my fiancé. I just don't want to fuck *you*, ASSHOLE! And what I do with my pussy is none of your fucking business. If I want to fuck my boss or every man in this damn coffee shop right now, it's none of your damn business!" I refute.

"Okay, chill out." He tries to calm me down, probably a little embarrassed seeing the other four or five patrons look up at us. "I'm sorry; I didn't mean to offend you. And you're right." He softens his voice and reaches for my hand again. "I just, I'm just going through a whole lot, Brit. And I miss you."

"Well I don't miss you. And I'm not interested. So if you'll excuse me, I have to get home." I get up to leave when I feel Anthony's strong arm reach out and grab me.

"Please? I mean, if you've already slept with Hogan, what does it matter if we fuck one last time? I'll even pay half the cost of the room." This man is a joke. Did he honestly think if I even agreed to this bullshit that I would be the one paying for *any* of the hotel room? He's still an extremely sad individual and I see now he is incapable of changing.

"No." I say coldly while looking him straight in the eye. That's when his macho, rude persona returns.

"Well, like I said, you spread your legs for Hogan. What's the difference between fucking him and fucking me?" He articulates loud enough for some of the coffee shop patrons to hear. I don't take offense; this man is obviously wounded. The little girl from *garbage* Dumois that used to jump at his beck and call and revere him as king, has suddenly come to her senses and is no longer interested. I am going to throw the same punch he threw my way months earlier. He wants to know what the difference is between fucking millionaire, Attorney William J. Hogan and fucking him... So I tell him:

"Opportunity." I respond loud and clear. As I place my Versace shades back on the bridge of my nose and elegantly walk out of Morehouse Coffee Shop without even looking back in his direction. I hop in my Mercedes and pull out of the parking lot feeling more powerful than Zeus. Check. Fucking. Mate.

Chapter 12: Once You Go Black...

~2000 Present Day~

I am convinced that saying has nothing to do with race, but was actually created to describe a dark state of mind. Once you go black (i.e. malevolent), there's no going back. I realize all my life I've been battling both my good and evil ways. If I had just accepted the fact that I was born to be bad from the beginning I would have avoided a lot of pain. Ever since I decided to take fate into my own hands and sleep with Hogan for career placement, and once I got over my initial regret period, I turned into a fearless and ambitious villain.

The old me would have never had the courage to reject Anthony the way I did three days ago. The old me would have never been able to afford taking my mother and Jeremy on a weekend trip to Osage Beach; one of the best beaches in Missouri. And the old me would definitely not be down here by the vending machines, boldly making googly eyes with Greg. I am living a consequence-free life and so far, so good. My motto is "win or learn", I don't believe in losing anymore. I don't believe there is a greater force with a white beard in the sky overseeing my destiny; I truly believe I am in control of my own destiny... It's almost magical how lately everything I think up has come to fruition. I like the new me, and I will continue to do what or whoever I want as long as it makes me happy. I will not allow society, *or my mother*, to dictate what appropriate behavior is for me. I wanted to fuck Deon Jackson (my mother's old neighbor), and I did. I wanted to fuck Bill Hogan, and I did. I wanted to fuck Burger Royale boy, and I did. I didn't want to fuck Anthony Johnson, and I didn't. Point is, no one is going to make me feel bad about the decisions I make regarding my life, because they are my decisions to make and live with.

This new, empowered woman I've become has been sweeping Greg off of his feet for the past couple of months. We've been eating lunch together almost every day since he's helped me get back on my feet the day I broke down outside of the office building.

Mid conversation, while I'm standing by the vending machines with Greg, I take a small wrapped gift out of my bag. "So anyways, I just wanted to say thank you and give you this to let you know I appreciated everything you've been doing for me lately." I hand him the gift.

"Wow, thank you." He smiles as he begins unwrapping. He stops when he realizes it's a box for a Rolex watch. "I can't even accept this." He shakes his head in the process of handing me back the box.

"I insist." I push his hand back towards him and away from me.

"No." He gets genuinely serious. "I really don't feel good accepting this, especially with everything I know about you." Over the past five months I have disclosed my deepest and darkest thoughts to Greg. He's stuck by my side as a true friend and he's been extremely non-judgmental. I've told him everything about the trip with Hogan, to the reason my mother and I had a falling out, to my adventures with Burger Royale boy, and I've even disclosed to him my entire journey with Anthony Johnson. I feel a deep connection with him, and even though I love Jeremey more than life itself, I can't help but feel the electricity brewing between Greg and me. So I did what my gut told me to do and bought him this expensive watch.

"Please take the watch. I engraved your name on the

back already; it's going to be a headache returning it." I insist.

"No." He is adamant about not taking the watch. "Everyone uses you Britney, I'm just trying to be your friend. Thank you, it means a lot to me, it really does. If they won't let you return it, take it back and tell them to engrave your fiancé's name over mine, rewrap it and give it to him instead."

"Okay." I sigh as I give up and put the watch back in my bag. I actually love Greg for that sentiment. This means whatever it is brewing between us is real. This means he's not just using me for money, possessions or my position. This means he might just genuinely care.

"Come here sweetheart, thank you." He says while pulling me into his tattooed arms, as he gives me a long tight hug. I love Greg's hugs, they make me extremely weak... *and wet*. He hasn't done anything to cross any boundaries since we kissed that one time in his car, and that happened before he even knew I was in a relationship at all. This is the first time, since Jeremy, that I've had a true sincere nonsexual friendship develop with a man.

"Well, I guess I'll make my way back upstairs. I have a lot to take care of." I say reluctantly cutting the hug short. If it were up to me, I'd be lost in the aroma of his sweet smelling cologne all day, but it isn't. I'm still on company time and my presence is sorely needed in order for work to get done, since Louisa is incompetent.

"Aw man!" Greg plays sad even though I know deep down he'll actually miss me. I know all this electricity isn't one sided, and remembering how passionate the kiss was that we shared almost eight months ago, I know he wants me just as bad.

"Yea... I know, so sad, but I have a question for you." I brace myself for possible rejection. "My fiancé is going out of town this weekend, meeting with TXA radio executives and I was just wondering if you'd like to spend time with me outside of work." Greg takes a second to think over the loaded question I just dropped on him. If he knows me as well as I think he does, he should know that was me offering up an invitation to finally fuck. He's already rejected the watch I purchased him, so I'm afraid he's going to reject my blatant advance next.

"Are you sure this is what you want to do?" He questions me, mistrustful of my emotional readiness.

"Yes. I really want you, and I respect you, and I know you respect me... I think we're ready to take it further." I reveal.

"I just don't want us to end up mad at each other if God forbid something goes wrong. And I definitely wouldn't want us bringing that drama here, to work, with us... Don't get me wrong Brit, I feel like I've already mastered your mind, so I would LOVE to explore your body... I just don't want to complicate things. Relationships always get messy when sex is involved, plus you used to be so fragile; I don't want you backtracking to where you used to be emotionally. I like the new, aggressive, and authoritative you." He mocks me as he makes a muscle arm. He's so dreamy; I can no longer control myself. I lean into him spontaneously, planting our second kiss onto his lips. I intend for it to be subtle and quick, since we are at work, but hidden feelings deep within the both of us are immediately unleashed. Greg pushes me against the nearest wall, pins both my arms on either side of me as he sticks his tongue deep within my mouth. His lips feel so fiery and intense; I even feel him rub his groin against mine. "Damn baby..." He breathes heavily as I push him off of me, afraid someone random would turn the corner at any moment and see us.

"This Saturday." I say seductively as I walk away. "This Saturday, be ready." I wink at him as I walk towards the elevators.

I am in cloud nine. I don't know if it's the motion of the elevator lifting me, or if it's just me being high off of my emotions, either way I feel as though I'm floating. On the way up, the elevator stops at the lobby and in enters Jane from accounting.

"You look extremely happy today Brit, Brit." She smirks.

"Oh, thanks for noticing, it's probably because I am." I bite back.

"I would be happy too if I was in an expensive ass, designer pant suit." She says matter-of-factly.

"Oh honey, you couldn't afford this. This right here is next year's Louie Verdone, *way* above your pay grade." I can't help but giggle to myself.

"Must be nice being the boss's ASS-sistant." She snaps back. The elevator stops on the third floor and she walks out.

"Oh Jane," I call after her. She turns around and faces me crossing her arms across her chest, feeling like she's won at life. "Just wanted to say you didn't have to worry your pretty little head. Bill and I are old news... But Greg, Greg is coming over this weekend, and when it comes to that bad boy... I can't make any promises." I wave as the elevator doors close in her face and take my bold ass up to my floor. I know how much Jane likes Greg, and I know that last statement is going to eat at her intestines.

When Louisa sees me approaching she immediately hangs up her phone. If this bitch thinks she's slick, call me an even *Slick*-er Rick. I walk straight towards her desk (which is my old, smaller desk), pick up her telephone and press the Redial button as Louisa timidly watches on.

"Hello?" A female voice I didn't recognize answers the phone. "Girl I thought you said your bitch ass boss lady who stole your job was coming back, I guess it was a false alarm huh? Good, cause that gossip you were giving me was on point."

"Oh, it was no false alarm. This is actually that bitch ass boss lady you were referring to. I just wanted to let you know, if you want your friend with all the juicy gossip, to not get written up for insubordination and possibly lose her job, then I suggest you advise her to refrain from calling you during work hours... especially from a recorded work line. Have I made myself clear?" I say into the phone when really I am looking into the depths of Louisa's eyes. She nods submissively while her friend on the other end of the phone just hangs up. For the past couple of months this girl has experienced how strict I have been when it comes to her foolishness. Hogan has given me complete control over Louisa, which means I have the power to terminate her employment if I see fit. You see, Hogan and Evica have always just had one legal secretary, no assistant. It's because Louisa couldn't handle the demands of the job that Evica decided to make up a job to help her cousin in the first place. That's how my old position was created; assistant to the legal secretary. No other legal secretary in the building has an assistant. Louisa's incompetence was why the job title was even created. Now that Evica and Bill have someone like me as lead secretary, who is capable of single handedly taking on the strenuous workload, Louisa has become nothing but dead weight to this firm. If it wasn't for Evica, Louisa would have been fired the moment the announcement was made that I got the promotion. Now that the poor girl is my subordinate, I am left in charge of her future with this company, and I treat her the same way she'd been treating me for the past three years.

After that unconventional warning, I make my way back to my desk (which is Louisa's old desk) and punch back in from lunch. I am turning into a powerful force not to be reckoned with, and this is all just the beginning.

~1996 Flashback~

"BABY I GOT THE JOB!" I screeched on the phone into Jeremy's ear.

"YES! That's GREAT news, Brit!" Jeremy genuinely sounded happier for me than I was for myself.

"It's only eight dollars an hour but in a year I promise to have saved enough for the down payment for those apartments in Tooley!"

"Aw baby, that would be amazing." I heard him chuckle. Jeremy and I were still living in our respective homes, twenty minutes away from each other in Dumois.

"I just can't wait to get out of public housing; I mean I've lived in this damn house for my whole life!" I whine.

"Just work hard and impress everyone like I know you will. When do you start?"

"Monday morning 9AM." I sing. "And get this, I told my mom about one of the partner's I interviewed with, the one who made fun of my sweater and Momma said she used to live right across the street from us... where the Jackson's live now! Their family supposedly moved out when I was five so I don't remember them at all."

"Well there you go, you should have someone to bond with since you both literally come from the same street." Jeremy laughed.

"Yea, you'd think... but she seems uppity and unapproachable. She was actually pretty rude to me during my interview. She treated me like I was beneath her. My mom says she's changed a lot since she's moved out of Dumois." I disclosed.

"Well just make sure you don't switch up on me like she did when you start hanging around all them rich folks. I already lost my brother to death; I don't want to lose my girlfriend to materialism." He said seriously.

"Aww baby, I won't ever change... I promise."

Chapter 13: Epiphany

~2000 Present Day~

It's 4AM, Saturday morning and I'm helping Jeremy load up a rented truck with tons of DJ equipment. My hard-working fiancé is on his way to Chicago, Illinois to meet with some TXA Radio Network executives. Poor thing has to drive about seven hours each way in order to make it on time for a two hour conference, which doesn't take place until early Monday morning. He probably won't make it back to Tooley until late Tuesday night, so hopefully this entire trip isn't in vain.

The TXA Radio Network was founded in 1973 and since then has purchased hundreds of radio stations all across North America. The network is just one branch of the most profitable TV and Radio media group in the country. They have produced and distributed everything from national news, talk radio, music radio (all genres), special event programs, local news, weather, video news, information radio, as well as traffic reporting services... Basically, they do it all. Now that Tooley is slowly developing into a renowned city, TXA execs are looking to buy out one of our dwindling local stations, and turn it into an area powerhouse. The network is currently searching for qualified individuals to fill potential job openings, and Jeremy is highly interested in being the Tooley branch's Music Director. Thanks to the impressive networking abilities, I exhibited at the Annual Business Gala, I was able to connect my baby directly with one of the network's top decision makers, and now, here Jeremy is on his way to formally interviewing for his dream job. My fiancé is one of the most popular DJs in the area with a decent sized fan base; his company, Bells Will Be Ringing, LLC has expanded in the past couple of months and covers everything from corporate gigs and weddings, to clubs and parties. This music director job would be right down his alley. I know how excited Jeremy, as a music lover, will be if he lands the title; plus, the position is very lucrative and will almost double our accumulated household income.

As soon as Jeremy pulls off, I race back into our apartment and begin to prepare for my long awaited date with Greg. Hair, make-up, clothes, nails, body waxing is all in motion… Tonight has to be perfect. My cell phone rings and it's Greg.

"Hello?" I answer, slightly out of breath from running around like a maniac.

"Hey, Sexy." I can hear it in his voice that Greg is smiling.

"You're the sexy one." I giggle.

"Just wanted to say I can't wait to see you tonight and also… there's no pressure to do anything." He's referring to sex. He knows my deepest secrets, and he knows more about my personality disorder than Jeremy does. "I just don't want you to feel obligated to do anything that might ruin how you view me."

"Aww… It's really sweet that you called me before our date to let me know all of this. I am actually flattered that you're considering my feelings and being so down to earth. So how about this? We go out, we have fun, and whatever happens, happens. I promise whatever I allow tonight is what I want." I confidently reply. I don't think Greg realizes that I've become a new woman ever since I received my promotion. I go for what I want with no regrets, and tonight what I want is him inside of me.

"Sounds like a plan." He coos, "See you at eight."

~Hours Later~

"Thank you." I say to Greg as he holds a door open for me. It's 8:20PM and we are walking inside Tooley's first and newly built Movie Theater. We are catching the 8:30PM viewing of the newest rendition of James Bond.

"You're very welcome." He smiles. I've never seen Greg wearing anything other than a mailroom uniform, so seeing him today with his own edgy and unique style is refreshing. Jane was right; he definitely has that 'irresistible bad boy' persona going for him. Ms. Accounting would probably die a slow death if she saw him and me at the movies together. Still thinking I have magical powers, I start wishing her into existence. I start focusing on her and hoping we bump into her somewhere tonight. After all, it worked the last time I wished I saw Anthony Johnson, and then BOOM he was at that gas station. So if I see Jane tonight it will validate my supernatural powers.

"This place looks so nice; I can't believe we're even in Tooley right now." I comment admiring the newly built high-tech theater. The smell of popcorn is tantalizing and I am tickled by all the noise and conversations going on. This place has only been open for about a week but by the looks of this crowd, it is already turning into the new hip, new hangout spot. I wish this was here when I was growing up, all we ever had around here was the Bowleria.

"Yea Tooley doesn't even look the same anymore." Greg rants, "Hopefully all this change is for the better."

"It definitely only gets better! When I was in DC, everything was beautiful, and the nightlife was poppin', so much culture and life…. I have a feeling we're going to turn into that." I excitedly disclose.

"True… But Mom and Pop stores are being shut down left and right, and too many out-of-towners can get really annoying. Plus, they increased the rent at my sister's apartments so now she's moving back to Dumois. It's like they're trying to keep all us poor folks out."

"You're right… Sorry about your sister. I'm trying to move my mother out of Dumois as soon as possible; it's getting worse and worse nowadays."

"That's nice, and my sister will be alright… But enough political talk now, we're on our long awaited first date," Greg laughs. "Only happy conversations and having fun are allowed from here on out." I nod in agreement. We get our snacks and make our way into room number 5 where our movie is playing.

This is truly the worst James Bond movie I've ever seen and I just finished all the popcorn. I feel fat because Greg bought us a large bucket and he barely got to eat two handfuls. I haven't been eating a lot regularly though, so this buttery cheat day was well deserved. I've already lost about 30 pounds and it's noticeable. It's getting cold in the theater and my nipples start to harden. I begin to feel frisky… Fuck this movie I want to be entertained another way. Luckily Greg and I are seated in the last row so I don't have to worry about being seen, I wipe my buttery hands off with a napkin and place my hand on Greg's lap.

Greg immediately loses focus on the movie as well. He turns his full attention to me as we begin wildly making out. I get bold and put my hand inside of his pants, for the first time I feel the complete outline of his penis. It's not that bad… He's substantially smaller than most of the men I've been with, but I don't let that ruin the mood. Who knows what motions he can bring into the bedroom to make up for his lack in girth? I am still extremely turned on despite Greg's size; he is kissing my neck and has just placed his hands on my breasts causing my breathing to accelerate.

"Want to get out of here?" I propose. Greg gets up to leave and grabs my hand without even bothering to verbally respond; I follow him out of the theater. When we get to his car we can't keep our hands off of each other. Even though I have the better car and higher income, he insisted on paying for the entire date and us riding in his car. I found those gestures sexy.

"Where are we headed?" He asks me between breaths.

"Vacation Inn." I respond while sucking on his neck.

We pull up to the Inn about twenty minutes later when I'm suddenly stricken by guilt. "I shouldn't have told you to come to this one."

"What's wrong with this one?" Greg inquires noticing my change in mood.

"Look, Greg... I want this to be different. I want us to be different. I don't know what this is yet, but I haven't felt like this since my fiancé. I'm not saying I want to leave him and run away with you, all I'm saying is I don't want to treat you like all the other men I've fucked in my past. This is where I'd take all of them and you deserve better than this." I say honestly.

"Ok, cool... We'll just go to another hotel." He turns his car back on and begins to pull out of the establishment's parking lot.

"No. I want to try something *completely* different... Let's go back to my apartment." I don't know what it was but something superstitious was telling me if I really cared about Greg, a hotel room shouldn't be the first place we make love. Every time I've fucked in a hotel room it's gone wrong. I didn't want this to feel like a booty call, this meant more to me. It's risky and extremely disrespectful to Jeremy bringing Greg back to my apartment, but at this very moment I feel like it's the right thing to do.

"Are you sure?" Greg is hesitant.

"Yes." I reply, he pulls off and drives a couple of blocks to the Tooley Towne Apartment Complex. He parks and we get out of the car and basically sprint to my floor and apartment. We are trying to avoid being seen by any nosey neighbors who might relay to Jeremy that I had another man in our home. (One neighbor in particular I am trying to avoid is Mrs. Williams. She's in her seventies and lives directly across the hall from us. Despite her age she's still as sharp as a thumbtack and nothing would go past her... Not to mention she treats Jeremy like a grandson).

Once safely in my apartment, I make sure to lock the door behind us and Greg and I go animalistic. We both shed

111

our clothes before we even make it to my bedroom. I take a second to take in Greg's naked body. He has more tattoos than I thought; he really is a beautiful specimen. His penis is fully erect but fairly disappointing to the eye. It doesn't lessen my emotions for him, I am still madly in lust with this man and excited about what our future together holds. He scoops me up and carries my naked body into my bedroom. He gently places me on my bed and spreads my legs. I can't believe this is happening; my dream was going to come true. Only thing missing about this moment is the vending machine... I close my eyes waiting to feel his wet tongue on my throbbing pussy, but instead, I feel his rough fingers and sharp finger nails. "OUCH!" I yell, caught off guard by the pain.

"Sorry." He says while pulling his fingers out of me. He gives up on my vagina and heads up to my breasts. He begins to circle his tongue around my erect nipples.

"Mm." I moan. Right when I start getting into the moment he chomps down hard on my nipple. "OW!" I yell again.

"Sorry." He says again. "I thought girls liked when guys nibbled on their nipples?"

"We do, but baby that was a bite... be gentler." I coach. He tries it again but still does it wrong. "OUCH GREG!" I am not feeling this foreplay at all.

"I'm so sorry, Brit." He looks embarrassed.

"It's okay, you're okay. Here, let me take over." I hint at Greg to go put on a condom so he reaches for his wallet which is laying on the floor and takes one out of it. He rips open the wrapper and throws it on the floor, then slides the latex on his dick. The condom is fairly baggy but I don't let it phase me. For me sex is mental and there's a strong enough connection between the two of us where I can look past his flaws. He gets back on the bed and lies on his back, I start to mount him while slowly sliding his penis inside of me. This is the smallest penis I think I've ever been with so I'm disappointed by how it feels inside of me, still I find a way to pleasure myself by rubbing on my clit while simultaneously beginning to bounce on his dick.

"OHHH FUCK!" Greg yells after only three or four strokes and he pushes me off him.

"What?" I ask puzzled.

"I came." He reveals, while getting up to discard the baggy condom filled with his semen. *What the fuck?* I think to myself. *That's it? This is what the fuck I've been waiting for?* Although I'm disappointed as hell, I don't show it. Greg is in the bathroom cleaning himself off and I'm just lying on the bed feeling like I'm in the twilight zone.

When he gets out of the bathroom he comes and lies down next to me. "I can stay the night right? I like to cuddle after sex." He smiles. His smile melts away my disappointment.

"Of course." I answer. We get under the covers and right before he falls asleep he kisses me on the cheek.

"Thanks baby girl… that was the best I've ever had. Was it good for you too?" He asks dozing off.

"Yea… yea… It was good baby." I lie. Greg knocks out less than a minute later. I stay up all night thinking about how horrible the experience was but how good he made me feel emotionally. I have flaws too and he's looked past them, I owe him a chance.

~The Next Morning~

Greg wakes me up at around 7AM, Sunday morning.

"Hey sleepy head." He is fully dressed. "I'm getting ready to head out, got to meet up with someone in a couple of hours."

"Oh. Ok." I am caught off guard.

"What's wrong?" He sees the sadness in my face.

"I just thought we might go grab breakfast or spend the rest of the weekend together." I honestly admit.

"Sorry Brit, no can do." He replies offering up no real explanation.

"It's fine." I lie, trying not to sound so clingy and mushy fast (which has ruined past relationships for me). "Well listen, do you want to come back later tonight and sleep

113

over again so we can ride into work together on Monday?"

"Uh…" Greg begins.

"What's wrong?" I ask confused.

"That's heavy Britney; we don't want to give off the wrong impression at work." He says and immediately a sharp pain runs all throughout my chest.

"THAT'S HEAVY?" I officially lose my cool. "THAT'S FUCKING HEAVY?" I get up from the bed, ass-naked.

"Whoa… Calm down. All I'm trying to say is we should just chill and go back to being friends. Plus, I wanted you to put in a good word for me with Hogan so I can get that mailroom supervisor position. He might not take you seriously if he thinks we're fucking." He says with a twisted facial expression.

"CHILL AND GO BACK TO BEING FRIENDS… MAILROOM SUPERVISOR POSITION?" I angrily imitate him. "ARE YOU FUCKING SERIOUS RIGHT NOW?"

"I don't know why you're getting so mad? This was supposed to be a fun, chill thing. That's why I couldn't accept the Rolex you gave me and I tried to warn you yesterday on the phone before we went out. I don't want anything heavy… Man, I knew you would switch up after the D."

"Switch up???" I am disgusted. "Greg, I'm not trying to be your girl or anything, I just want us to be the friends we've been. You used to give me rides all the time."

"Yea… When you didn't have a car." He looks disturbed.

"Last night you gave me a ride to the movies?" I argue.

"Yea but we weren't at work… look, it's just heavy. You have a man, you already fucked Hogan so do you really want to be sexually connected to *another* man at work? I'm doing this for your own good. We can still chill outside of work from time to time, I'm just trying to help your reputation out."

"GET THE FUCK OUT!" At this point I am belligerent and my tears are uncontrollably falling from my eyes. "GET THE FUCK OUT OF MY APARTMENT NOW!" I scream throwing Greg's wallet and car keys at him. Without another peep Greg grabs his stuff and leaves. I get back in bed and cry myself to sleep for the rest of the day.

~Two Days Later~

It's Tuesday evening and I called out of work yesterday and today. I am in pain and sick from heartbreak. I haven't heard from Greg, nor have I called him for the past two days. I haven't even left my apartment or showered since Greg has been here. I've had very little food, I can't even eat for real, and my stomach is in knots. I really thought he was different. I have been replaying the whole ordeal over and over in my head. What did I do wrong? What do I always do wrong? I suddenly hear keys at the front door and realize Jeremy was due back from Chicago around this time. I quickly wipe the tears from my eyes and switch up into a perkier mood. I can't show him any signs of heart ache.

"BABY!!!" I scream excitedly as I run to meet him at the door.

"Hey mama, I missed your little sexy ass." He lifts me as I run to him. "What's wrong?" He immediately notices my red puffy eyes.

"I've been sick. I think I have food poisoning." I lie. "I've been home from work for the past two days."

"Aww… poor baby." He puts his keys down and carries me to our room. He lovingly unrobes me with no sexual intentions and begins to rub my back. "Did you eat anything?" He coos as he leaves light kisses on my back.

"I should be asking you that Jer. You're the one who just drove a million hours to get back home, how was the interview by the way?" I inquire.

"I have no idea, won't know for a while. They're not even all the way sure that they're going to buy a station here so everything is hush." He looks exhausted. "But I'm not going to let any of that bring me down, if it's meant for me, God will make it happen. Whatever door he opens no man can close." He smiles. I suddenly realize how beautiful and

115

positive my fiancé is. I can't believe how bad I've been treating him behind his back.

"I don't deserve you." I unintentionally blurt out.

"Don't ever say that again." Jeremy scolds me as he continues to rub and kiss my back. "I love you; you're my everything… And no, I'm not hungry. I just wanted to come home and get in bed with you and sleep the night away. I'm so tired from driving. I ate on the way home so I'm fine."

"Okay." I exhale. I am so extremely comfortable. There's nowhere safer than his arms. "I really don't know what I'd do without you."

"Dido." Jeremy then gets in bed next to me and passes out. Meanwhile I am guilt stricken and my heart hurts. I didn't even have the audacity to change the sheets Greg and I soiled. I vowed to never hurt Jeremy again for as long as I lived. I got up and took my phone into the restroom and locked the door. Sitting on the toilet seat I began to delete every male number in my phone book. I made a covenant to myself that from this moment on I would be a new and improved me. Never will I ever cheat on my king again.

Chapter 14: Business as Usual

~2000 Present Day~

It takes everything in me to hop out of my parked Mercedes. I haven't been at work for the past two days and even though it lifted my spirits to have Jeremy back home with me last night, I am still very much emotionally drained. I dread bumping into Greg at work today; I need at least a month of recovery time before I see him again. I need to heal from this knot I have in the pits of my stomach created by him. In all my years with Hogan & Wildes, LLP; the past couple of days were the first instances of me *ever* calling out.

When the elevator doors open up on the fifth floor, the first thing I see is Hogan walking around yelling like an animal. "...THIS DELUGA CASE FILE WAS SUPPOSED TO BE PREPARED FOR ME BY MONDAY, IT'S NOW WEDNESDAY AND IT'S STILL NOT DONE!" He is now hovering over Louisa, reprimanding her.

"I-- I was working on it-- Mr. Hogan--- B-B-Britney's been sick." I hear a meek Louisa stutter from under him.

"I'm here, I'm here." I jump in, in an attempt to defuse the situation.

"*Thank God.*" Louisa mouths under her breath.

"Sorry team, I was really sick with that stomach virus." I lie. I used that same cover up story with Jeremy. "I'm here now; I'll take care of everything."

"You'd better." Hogan mumbles as he stomps back into his office. Evica, who is observing everything from down the hall, retreats back into her own office as well. There are still a small number of lawyers peeking from their office windows.

"The hell Britney, you know damn well I couldn't prepare that file case on my own, you called out on purpose to see me sink." Louisa croaks before I even have the chance to get situated at my desk.

"Look... I was sick, okay? But who cares now, I'm here and I'll take care of it." I say while rolling my eyes at her.

"I care!" Louisa storms over to my desk. "Do you know how humiliating it is to be yelled at like that in front of the entire fucking office?" I can see the tears forming in her eyes. "It's bad enough I got demoted and you took my job, but now everyone thinks I'm a fucking idiot!"

"Louisa calm down, number one, nobody thinks you're an idiot, and number two, I understand you're angry, but don't ever curse at me again. For your information I didn't do this on purpose to embarrass you, my life doesn't revolve around you and this job, I really wasn't feeling well... If you'd like you can scoot your chair into my desk area and I'll show you how to quickly and efficiently prepare a case file, that way next time you can do it on your own."

"Fuck that." She says going back to her desk where she pulls out her cell phone.

"Well then just work on your own thing, but you're going to have to put that phone away." I firmly relay.

"I'm texting Evica." Louisa's tone is filled with hatred.

"Okay, well can you please either walk down the hall to her office and tell her whatever you have to tell her, or wait until you go on your break before using your cell phone? You know our policy here; I don't even have my cell out because we have sensitive client information out everywhere; plus, it's just unethical to handle personal business on the company's time." I calmly reiterate to her our company policy.

"LEAVE ME ALONE BRITNEY, YOU'RE WORKING MY NERVES." Louisa barks.

"Put away your phone, and if you talk to me like that again I'm writing you up." I repeat adding a little more authority to my tone.

"No." She spews venomously.

"Well then... I'm going to Bill's office to let him know you're being insubordinate." Louisa stand's up as soon as I finish my statement.

"FUCK YOU! FUCK HOGAN! FUCK THIS COMPANY! AND FUCK MY FAKE ASS COUSIN WHO DIDN'T EVEN STAND UP FOR ME OR HELP ME FIGHT

118

TO KEEP MY POSITION!" At this point, everyone on our floor is out of their offices listening in on an out of control Louisa. "THIS IS BULLSHIT AND I'M NOT TAKING IT ANYMORE, NOT FROM YOU, NOT FROM HOGAN, AND NOT FROM EVICA." After she ends her rant Louisa grabs her cell phone, a bonsai plant, and picture frames that were on her desk and throws them all into a box she had ready under her desk. Without saying another word, Louisa storms to the staircase and begins making her way off of the premises. A frantic Evica appears out of nowhere and follows her cousin out, possibly in an attempt to calm her down and change her mind. I am secretly hoping that lazy leach is really gone for good; she did absolutely nothing for the betterment of this company.

Unfazed by the whole ordeal I grab a cup of coffee and get adjusted in my office chair, right before I am about to open up the enormous Deluga file on my desk, the office phone rings; it's Bill.

"Hello?" I answer it.

"Come to my office." And then suddenly, *click* just like that he hangs up. I walk over to Hogan's office a little irritated by him summoning me knowing damn well I had a lot of work to complete on my desk.

When I get to his door it is already open so I let myself in. "What's up?" I ask casually as I seat myself in one of the spare chairs in his enormous office.

"Wow, the new money has made you really relaxed." Bill snarls.

"Or maybe it was the sex… Or the fact that I've been busting my ass for this company going on close to four years now… So I feel somewhat entitled to feeling *relaxed*." I snarl back.

"Uh… Okay." He is shocked by my bluntness, but he doesn't argue it because I've stated nothing but facts. "Did Louisa leave?" Hogan asks ignoring my attitude and changing the subject.

"Yep, and Evica ran after her… She'll be back though." I laugh.

"No she won't." Bill says sternly. "I already sent an email to human resources, she is no longer allowed in this building."

"Wow." I say emotionless.

"Britney, be a doll and clean out her desk." He orders as I get up to walk out of his office, assuming that was the end of the conversation.

"Sure, I'll get to it before the weekend." I say while almost halfway out the door.

"I'm actually going to need that done by this afternoon." Hogan further instructs, stopping me in my tracks.

"Really? Why the rush, I'm sure the desk isn't going anywhere." I joke, turning back around to face him.

"Because… Her replacement, Jasmine Hall, will be here early tomorrow morning." He smirks.

"Wow! That was fast." I comment somewhat impressed by his speediness.

"We can't dwell on people who aren't helping this firm move in an upward direction. You'll be happy to know it won't be necessary to train this young lady, she already knows the ropes and has worked for a firm before. Evica is going to be running around here angry but I've made up my mind. I wish Louisa the best in her future endeavors, but tomorrow we're back; business as usual." With that I walk back to my desk feeling kind of morbid. The words 'business as usual' struck up an old and painful memory:

~1994 Flashback~

A month after I broke up with Anthony Johnson for not committing to me (before I knew about him and Tina); I waited patiently outside of the mall for him to get off of work. I had been trying to contact him for weeks prior to that day with no response, so his actions drove me to behaving like a stalker.

"Why have you been ignoring me?" I remember asking him as soon as I saw him. He was walking out with a group of co-workers when he spotted me and stopped in his tracks. Ignoring me he said goodbye to everybody and proceeded to walk to a bus stop across the street. "Hello? Stop ignoring me!" I fast walked after him.

"Girl, you broke it off with me, remember?" He laughed.

"Because you weren't trying to take me serious, you make me feel like all I'm good for is sex, bringing you lunches, and buying you things!" I remember starting to cry uncontrollably.

"Well… You made yourself available." He shrugged.

"Damn! Why the fuck is you so cold?" I yelled.

"Look… I'm not ready for a relationship, girl. I'm too young and so are you. You're only about to be twenty-one years old, why the fuck would you want that kind of commitment? I like what we had, but you got too serious and shit, I don't need the extra stress… I think we should've just had fun." He brushed me off and continued to walk towards the bus stop (back then neither of us drove). To my horror the bus he needed to board was pulling up, but I wasn't satisfied with our conversation. I needed more time and I wasn't about to get on this bus with him, we lived in opposite directions and it was getting late.

"PLEASE DON'T GET ON THAT BUS!" I recall begging him as he started to walk towards it. "ANOTHONY I'LL SUCK YOUR DICK IF YOU DON'T GET ON THAT BUS." I yelled after him in desperation, hoping that would convince him to miss his damn bus. I knew Anthony couldn't resist a good blow job, and according to him, I gave the best ones he'd ever had. He stops in his tracks, turns around, and begins (for the first time that night) to walk towards me. The bus ended up driving past us.

"What, girl?" He acted nonchalant knowing damn well he missed my lips around his dick. I grabbed his arm and took him to a desolate area behind the bus stop. I hungrily unzipped his pants knowing I'd been craving that man for the past couple of weeks. My plan failed drastically, a month ago I thought he would fold and be the one to call me if I stood my ground and left him. I did so well for a whole week after I initially ended things, but I couldn't last, I started blowing up his phone and sending him millions of emails. If I didn't go confront him that day at the mall, he probably never would have agreed to speak with me again. "Mm." He moans as my tongue hit the head of his penis. I looked up at him and saw him biting his lip in pleasure. I proceeded to suck him dry. I didn't care that I sporadically heard random footsteps on the sidewalk not far from where we were hidden, and neither did he. We were both in bliss. I felt my pussy throbbing. Prior to that day I wanted nothing more than to taste him again, and I finally was. I remember I used to be able to attain an orgasm just by sucking Anthony's dick, that's how intense the sex was. My goody-two-shoes, ex-boyfriend David never made me feel the way Mr. Anthony Johnson did. I was completely dick sprung by him. He tasted the sweetest he ever had that day, I recall madly sucking on each one of his balls before jamming his entire manhood down my throat. I didn't gag once, I basically swallowed his dick whole. His moans became louder and louder every time my lips went down on his shaft. I knew it was only a matter of time before he came. I could always tell when Anthony was about to reach his peak by how he'd start firmly gripping the back of my head and pulling it towards him, this would cause his penis to go deeper down into my throat. His breathing increased and became heavier before he finally lost his mind and exploded in my mouth. "FUCK!" He let out a final cry as I swallowed every single drop.

Getting off my knees I used my shirt's sleeve to wipe the dripping saliva from around my mouth, the head had been extremely sloppy. "Damn girl, that was great. I forgot how amazing that shit felt." He laughed as he put his penis away and zipped up his pants.

"Can we talk now?" I asked.

"Okay but make it quick, there's another bus coming in a couple of minutes." He stated.

"Damn, I just did all that and I can't get longer time?"

"I feel like we already talked about everything we need to. You and I want different things." He said turning back into the guy that he was before I gave him head. "I want this kind of fun, and you want me to marry you and shit." He laughed.

"Not true, I don't want you to marry me or anything right now; I just want to know that you'd consider it for our future if I committed myself to you. There's a lot of boys I could be messing with but I only fuck with you, I want to know that if we stay together I'll be good when I'm in my late twenties. Don't you want a wife... and a family? Anthony, can't you imagine an Anthony Jr.?" I try appealing to his softer side.

"Listen Brit, I don't feel right wasting your time. I don't want to get married, I probably never will. I'm a pimp, a player... I have fun!" He taunted my dreams of a future together. Looking back, I know now he was lying because five months after this conversation he was walking down an aisle with someone else. I know now it wasn't that he didn't want to get married, it was that he just didn't want to get married to *me*. For all I know, he had most likely already started talking to Tina by that time and I had just sucked his dick like an idiot while he went home to spend hours on the phone with her preppy, rich ass.

"So what now... Just throw away the past year?" I wept uncontrollably.

"Why you got to say it like that, Brit? We had fun... It's been cool. It really has, it's just... Now it's back to business as usual."

"Back to *'business as usual'* huh?" I solemnly repeated his icy words as the next bus pulled up.

"Bye girl." Anthony said as he boarded the bus. And that was that, the rest is written.

~2000 Present Day~

It's Thursday, and I just made it to the office. While getting out of my car I see a new face by the entrance of the building. It's a cute girl with a petite figure and a head full of curls. I could tell she used public transportation to get here by her dress and sneakers combination.

"Jasmine?" I assume while walking towards her.

"That's me!" She smiles so friendly and perky.

"Hi, I'm Britney, Bill and Evica's lead legal secretary. Welcome to the team!" I extend my arm for a handshake.

"Girl, come in here." She laughs as she pulls me in for a full blown hug. I like her personality already, different from a lot of the women here. Hopefully she stays this friendly.

"Well let me take you upstairs and show you your desk, and then after you speak with the boss man I'll take you on a tour of the whole building."

"Sounds awfully nice." She gives me another big smile. "By the way, I love your suit! It's beautiful, and your make-up is flawless!" She genuinely compliments me; at this point I am convinced she's a God send. For the past year I've been praying for a friend at work, I'm hoping she's the answer to my prayers. "...I can't believe I'm going to actually be working here at the infamous Hogan & Wildes law firm." She shrieks.

"Yea, it's great, isn't it?"

Chapter 15: The New Girl

~2000 Present Day~

It's only been three weeks since Jasmine Hall's first day at the firm but it feels like I've known her my whole entire life. I don't know what it was that made me open up to her, maybe it was my years of longing for female companionship, but I am ever so grateful for her. I told her everything about my life, she knows almost as much as Greg knows, if not more because I've talked to her about Greg. Hell, but I know for a fact she knows way more about the real me than Jeremy does. She makes me feel comfortable and unashamed of being myself because she has also shared some demeaning things about herself as well.

Jasmine told me things like she was molested as an adolescent by her uncle and that now as an adult, she was addicted to male attention. Aside from the tragic child abuse, I feel like we have the male attention thing in common. She also told me where she lives, which is literally two blocks from my mother's house in Dumois. Since I've met her, Jasmine constantly lets me know how I inspire her and how she wants to move up in the firm, and in salary, like I did. I let her drive my Benz on her break and she would do sweet things for me like have a hot chocolate mocha on my desk before I got in. It also helps that her work ethic is the complete opposite of Louisa's, Hogan was right, this chic knows what she's doing and has definitely worked at a firm before. She helped me complete the Deluga file and has taken seventy-five percent of my workload off me. I can't say one bad thing about her, I honestly can't.

~Two Weeks Earlier~

I knew I could completely trust her when she stood up for me against my worst nightmare. It had just been a week after Louisa quit, and Jessica and I were both giggling on our way back from lunch. We were waiting in the lobby to catch an elevator back to the fifth floor when the doors opened up revealing Greg standing beside a co-worker of his. That's when I completely froze, it was the first time I had seen him since the day I kicked him out of my apartment and my stomach was in knots. Up until that point I had done a great job of avoiding him at all costs.

"Hello ladies." The other mailroom clerk said flirtatiously (obviously in the dark about the awkward history I had with his friend).

"Hi." I responded abruptly. My throat was drier than a desert in August, my palms were sweaty, my voice cracked... I was just a really big mess. Jasmine must have read my body language because she immediately jumped to my rescue.

"Hey fellas!" She sang trying to cut at the awkwardness of the moment.

"How are you on this beautiful day?" He continued while Greg and I stayed silent. The men began to exit the elevator as Jasmine and I boarded it; Greg's co-worker placed his hand on one of the elevator doors, keeping them from shutting as he waited for a response.

"We're good, just coming back from lunch." Jasmine responded politely.

"You must be new." Greg finally chimed in completely ignoring my presence and speaking over me towards Jasmine.

"I am." She said as her smile faded.

"I'm Greg." He reached out his arm and she reluctantly shook his hand. "Aren't you going to tell me your name?" He continued. I felt a dagger pierce through my heart, was he the same Greg I knew from before our awful encounter? Was this the guy that was all over me only weeks earlier?

"No, I'm alright." She scoffed.

"Damn girl, it's like that?" Greg chuckled trying to play off being shut down in front of his friend, who had been standing in the middle of it all chuckling immaturely.

"Yep." Jasmine stood her ground.

"Why? Cause *that girl* told you something about me?" He spat in my direction. It was the first time that Greg even acknowledged me during the entire conversation and he just

126

referred to me as 'that girl'? *Wow*... I immediately gave him a stern look as if to say SHUT THE FUCK UP, GREG!

The truth was that back then I hadn't even told Jasmine about Greg yet, but because he'd just been shut down he was trying to blame that rejection on me. I had nothing to do with that, she wasn't interested on her own, and I didn't appreciate how he was treating me. I held my tongue because I didn't want my business out in the office, but I mentally planned on giving him a call once I got off from work that day and cursing his ass out. Jasmine must have read my mind because she came to my rescue again and said: "No. I don't know you, never heard of you and Britney and I have never even talked about you, but you see, she didn't have to... I peeped for myself how you just tried to play her." She let out venomously. "Dude's like you with your tattoos and your edgy immature haircuts act all *bad*, but really you're just really insecure and childish. Judging by your threads you couldn't even afford a girl like me anyways." She cackled referring to his mailroom uniform. Secretly ecstatic about how she put Greg in his place, I began violently pressing the door close button from the inside of the elevator because I didn't want to bust out laughing right there in Greg's face.

"Bougie bitch." He replied to Jasmine under his breath as his friend stopped propping the doors open, suddenly realizing the seriousness of the situation.

"Kiss my ass." Jasmine shouted back at him as the elevator doors finally closed. That was when I knew this girl had my back. That was the day I ended up eventually telling her everything about Greg and I, Hogan and I, and Jeremy and I. I told her EVERYTHING, and since then we've been inseparable. It feels really good to have my first *real* female friend, let alone to have one at work.

~2000 Present Day~

Anyways, today is a special day, I turn twenty-seven and I just arrived at work. When I get to my desk it is laced with balloons, candy, and a card. Of the past three birthdays I've spent with this company, this is the first one celebrated,

127

so I instantly realize it has to be Jasmine's doing. I look over at her as tears fill my eyes. "OH MY GOD! THANKS GIRL!" I walk towards her desk and squeeze the life out of her with a monster hug.

"Aww... No problem Sweets, I wanted to do something special for you." She smiles.

"This is more than something *special.* It's very, very sweet and unexpected." I add, sincerely touched by the sentiment.

"That's not it! Read your card!" She eggs me on.

"Okay..." I grin as I open up the card on my desk. I laugh at the comedic message beautifully printed on the outside and as soon as I open it up, out falls two tickets to see Homeboy Duggar. "Wow, I've heard of him... isn't he a rapper?" I try to sound cool knowing damn well I knew nothing about this generation's music.

"Not only is he a rapper, he's *the* BIGGEST rapper out now! He's done songs with everyone from Michael Jackson to Destiny's Child and he made it on this year's Forbes list, which means he's fucking loaded!" Funny how Jasmine is way more excited about the gift she got me than I am, regardless I really appreciate the gesture. "Anyways, those aren't just regular tickets girl; those are the best seats in the house!" She shrieks.

"Wow! How much did this cost? I can't accept this!" I say surprised.

"It's cool girl, I got them for the low. I had to fuck an old friend in order to come across them, but he gave them to me at a ridiculously low price." She laughs. I can't help but laugh along with her at her brutal honesty. "Anyways the show is tomorrow night!"

"Tomorrow is a Wednesday." I say a little skeptical about going.

"...And?" She gives me a sneering glare, "Just because you're a year older today doesn't mean you're fifty! We both don't have any kids, we're both still in our twenties, and we both deserve this awesome night out." She pep talks me into being fully on board.

"Alright." I sigh, "I'm in!"

I can't believe I am out on a work night at a rap concert; Jasmine brings out the party girl in me. It's almost one in the morning and we are both screaming at the top of our lungs towards a stage. This Homeboy Duggar guy isn't half bad, turns out I've heard a lot of his music on the radio but I just didn't put a name to the sound. Jasmine made me wear something sleek and sexy and we drove together here in my Mercedes; I picked her up from her house in Dumois. We were both wearing short ass white dresses. According to Jasmine, the white would illuminate in the dark crowd, and since we were front-row-center Duggar would have no choice but to notice us.

A year ago I would have never been caught dead in this dress, but after losing about forty pounds total since I first got promoted, I am in the best shape I have ever been in my entire life. My 125lb body is banging, and the best thing about it is I was able to keep all of my curves in all the right places. We both looked great. Jasmine is a pretty girl and she looks the best I'd ever seen her look tonight. I never noticed how big her ass was until I saw her in this dress, I usually have the biggest ass almost everywhere I go, but tonight we were both bulging out of our tight dresses. My weight loss did nothing to change my cup size, my boobs are still huge and are much bigger than hers, but to me her face is prettier than mine. Her big curly hair is swaying back and forth to the music; I feel the eyes of all the guys in our section on us. I can't really move the way I want to because I feel slightly insecure standing next to Jasmine even though I think we are almost equally beautiful. She definitely stands out by having all the latest dance moves down packed.

Homeboy Duggar is running up and down the stage when I feel him look in our direction. "EEP!" I hear Jasmine screech above the already loud music. "He's looking at us, girl! COME HERE!" That's when Jasmine grabs me and starts to kiss me.

129

"What the fuck?" I back up startled.

"No." Jasmine laughs, "Trust me, I don't want you." She yells in my ear. "I want him, and he'll want us if you play along." She explains, so I agree to go along with her wishes.

"Okay just don't kiss me on the lips." I scream back at her. She nods and continues to fend for Duggar's attention. Jasmine starts to hold me and grabs my round soft ass as the rapper looks on from the stage. She starts smacking my ass, I do the same to hers and we start to rub chests against each other. Damn, we not only have the attention of the rappers, but looking up at the jumbo screen we have the attention of the whole arena.

"We're on the jumbo screen!" Jasmine jumps up and down pointing towards the mega screen behind the stage. She starts smiling towards the camera and unexpectedly takes off her bra from underneath her dress, shimmies her chest, and proceeds to throw her bra on stage at the rapper and his entourage.

"NOW THAT'S HOW WE PARTY!" Duggar yells into the microphone as his fans in the audience go wild. I must admit, I love all the attention. Jasmine is fun as hell.

When the concert ends and Jasmine and I are making our way back to my car, security stops us. "Excuse me ladies." A buff man says, "Do you mind following me?" He adds.

"Uh… yes, what the fuck did we do?" Jasmine hisses. That's when the enormous man whispers something into her ear and Jasmines tone completely changes. "Well why the fuck didn't you say that from the beginning?" She smiles, "after you". She motions at the guard to walk ahead of us. She grabs my arm and we begin following him through a door that has a sign on it which reads: Staff Only.

"Where are we going?" I whisper into Jasmine's ear.

"Girl! We are fucking meeting the band!" She shrieks.

"Wow", I whisper back. "That's awesome." And I keep walking. The door takes us all the way to the back of the stadium to an enormous dressing room.

"Is this Duggar's dressing room?" Jasmine asks the security man, who by the way looks exactly like Dwayne "The Rock" Johnson.

"Yep, Homeboy and his crew will meet y'all here in a couple of minutes. Would you like any weed or alcohol in the meantime?" He asks all nonchalantly.

"NO!-YES!" Jasmine and I answer differently at the same time.

"Why no?" Jasmine grills me.

"Um... because it's almost 3AM and we have to BE at work in less than six hours." I state the obvious.

"Girl, the night is still young, and so are we!" She laughs. "I'm ready to GO WILD!" She screeches.

"I'll bring you ladies some of both." The Rock look-a-like grins as he leaves us in the room together. Half an hour later he returns with our drinks and Duggar and his boys are still nowhere in sight. Jasmine begins rolling up some weed and pours us two shots of vodka.

"No thanks." I roll my eyes as she attempts to hand me a glass.

"Girl loosen up; this is a once in a lifetime opportunity." She explains, exasperated by my unwillingness to partake in night's the festivities.

"I'm just not comfortable drinking when I have to be up for work, plus I don't exactly trust the intensions of these rappers." I share.

"Whatever... more for me." Jasmine then shoots back

both shots of liquor and lights her jay. "Fuck your little attitude; *I'm* going to party tonight." Jasmine laughs. Immediately after she ends her sentence Homeboy Duggar and a group of five other men waltz into the dressing room.

"LADIES! WHAT'S UP? WHAT'S UP?" Duggar yells from the door.

"OH MY GOD! Am I dreaming?" Jasmine springs up and runs to the door. "I can't believe it's really you guys! I loved the show tonight." She turns into putty in their hands while I remain seated.

"Well we enjoyed *y'all* show." Duggar smiles, he's referring to Jasmine and I getting freaky for the jumbo screen. *Oh God*, at this point I am ready to go home.

"Well that was all for you daddy." Jasmine says turning into a complete slut. I'm all for being sexy and craving attention, but I am a mostly private person. I don't like group sex or being a groupie. I've never been in a threesome and I've only had one on one, private encounters (not including the time I let my mother's neighbor watch).

"Your home girl doesn't seem as excited as you," Duggar heckles in my direction. "It's cool though, I like 'em hard to get."

"I'm not '*them*'." I hiss.

"Wow, very feisty. But I saw your little display of affection for me earlier; I know you'll be mine by the end of the night." He speaks ever so confidently. Not only am I holding out because I made a pact with myself to leave my ho-ish ways behind since the day I fucked Greg in my apartment, but I am also completely turned off by the antics of Duggar and his crew. I am also disappointed in my girl Jasmine, usually she's all about me and making me feel comfortable, but right now it's like she's turned a switch and is permanently stuck on groupie mode.

"I'm engaged." I say annoyed.

"I don't see a ring," Duggar eggs on. "You aren't the only groupie that takes their rings off during our concerts." Just then everybody in his crew busts out laughing, including Jasmine. I ignore Duggar and his 'yes men' and proceed to pull out my cell phone and play in it, ignoring everyone in the room. Once Duggar realizes I wasn't playing with him, he and his crew start to focus on Jasmine. I swear the room just turned into a porno and they all are neglecting the fact that I'm sitting right here. They all start to get extremely freaky right in my presence.

A dude from Duggar's crew starts to smack and grip Jasmine's ass while another starts to lower the front of her dress exposing her breasts. *Oh my God*, I think to myself. This girl is really about to let six guys touch all over her? It doesn't stop there, a third member of the crew starts sucking on her breasts. I want to look away but I've never seen this type of shit in person so I can't help but look on. It is all turning me on and disgusting me at the same time, but nonetheless I have ZERO desire in joining in.

At this point Jasmine is completely naked. The dress must have been a miracle worker because her body isn't as great as I expected. She has a lot more stretch marks than I do on her belly and her boobs fell flat as soon as the dress came off.

"I'll suck anyone, but I only want Duggar to fuck me." Jasmine moans out her wishes, by this point I can't even see her, she's surrounded by men with their pants down to their ankles.

"You heard the lady." Duggar laughs and proceeds to move behind Jasmine, bending her over. He motions for a condom from one of the guys in his entourage, grabs it, and places it on. Jasmine starts to scream as he starts fucking her in front of everyone. A couple more girls enter through the same doors that Jasmine and I had come in from. Some look timid and confused, while others jump right in with Jasmine and strip down naked. The room becomes an enormous orgy. All six men are having sex with different women at the same time. I am focused on my phone most of the time but the last time I looked up, I saw Duggar fucking Jasmine from the back and pulling on her wild curly hair while another guy squeezed her breasts while she gave him head. This girl parties extremely too hard, even for me. I am ready to leave.

About a half hour later I hear Duggar finally cum all over Jasmine's ass. "Finally." I say under my breath.

"Can I call you sometime?" Jasmine sounds pathetic as she asks Duggar for his number.

"Girl, bye." Duggar laughs as he zips up his pants and exits the room without even looking back at her. Jasmine yells obscenities after him as she stumbles towards me. She pours herself another shot of vodka and downs it.

"I'm ready to go." She slurs her words. I get up and we start walking out. I don't say one word to the girl, even during the entire car ride dropping her off at her house in Dumois. "Well I had fun, how about you?" She asks me reeking of weed and alcohol.

"*Real* fun, thanks." I lie. I wait and make sure Jasmine enters her house before driving off. I look down at the clock in my dashboard; it reads 6:12AM. I'm going to be tired as fuck tomorrow at work. "That bitch." I say to myself as I drive back to Tooley in silence.

Chapter 16: The Calm before the Storm

~2000 Present Day~

    I can't believe I was able to wake up for work. It is storming outside and the weather is matching my mood. I just arrived at work and I feel so drowsy. I'm surprised I didn't fall asleep on the drive in. Not only did I get home at 6:30AM but I stayed up an extra hour explaining to Jeremy the horrors of what happened. I am so glad I left the 'ho life' behind me because I would hate to ever end up like Jasmine.

    Evica is by my desk with an evil look on her face. "You're late." She snaps at me.

    "Only by thirty minutes, Evica… I had a long night." I explain too tired to get into details.

    "Well your new co-worker has completely messed up the files in my office; she throws them in recklessly and now they're not alphabetical. How the fuck am I supposed to operate in that mess?" She continues to bark at me.

    "Where is she?" I ask referring to Jasmine.

    "Who knows? Every time I see that girl around the building she's either flirting with security or sitting on a lawyer's desk with her legs wide open." Evica explains, "My cousin wasn't as educated as everyone here, but she damn sure wasn't a hussy. The last thing this law firm needs is another hussy." Evica spews, not making eye contact with me. Did this woman just call me a hussy? I chuckle silently; I'm too tired to fight this battle. I decide to set off and look for Jasmine. She is going to fix the files she messed up, she isn't Louisa, she didn't have a family member in high places, I am not about to do her work for her.

    I decide to start my search for Jasmine in the basement, I remember Hogan telling her to send out packages for him yesterday before we left work. I remember she put those packages to the side promising to send them off early this morning. Once in the basement I walk in the mailroom. Greg is there working with two other clerks.

    "What do you want?" He barks before I can even speak.

"I'm just looking for Jasmine." I say exasperated. Again, I am way too tired to fight these battles. I'm operating on less than an hour of sleep.

"Well she already was down here and left, so you can go back up with her."

"Damn, why are you giving me all this attitude?" I ask annoyed at how he's been treating me for the past couple of weeks.

"Because it's not womanly of you to send your home girl down here to attack me with her smart mouth. Why are you allowing her to disrespect me? You know I know too damn much about you, don't make me write a tell all." He croaks.

"First of all, I didn't send anyone down here to attack you; I don't even know what you're talking about." I say, honestly confused.

"Of course you don't. I asked around about Jasmine, she's only been here less than a month and she already fucking a lot of the lawyers. You sure do know how to pick your friends. I guess my broke ass wasn't enough for her. You and she are a lot alike. You know what they say, birds of a feather…" With that all three men burst out laughing. I cannot believe Greg, my once best friend just came out in front of a group of people and called me a ho!

"Greg, I didn't do anything to you, please stop."

"Oh, so now we didn't do anything? So you telling me I didn't have you on your back a couple of weeks ago?" He says twisting my words.

"Look… FUCK YOU!" At this point I'm exhausted and both my patience and reasoning fly out the window. "I don't know where this entire attitude is coming from but it needs to stop." I order him.

"Or else what? You'll get the other guy you're fucking in this building to fire me?" That was the last straw.

"For your fucking information you broke ass wanna-be mailroom clerk supervisor, I do have the power and influence to get you the fuck out of here, don't test me. And as far as me and you fucking is concerned, it was the worst

136

fucking sex I've ever had in my ENTIRE life and for me to be a big time 'ho' that's saying A LOT. Out of all the dicks I've ever had, yours was the smallest and weakest, at least Hogan put in that work, your shit? I couldn't even feel! Not to mention you came fast as shit. THREE STROKES? Come the fuck on!" I spew out the truth.

"Stop lying." Greg tries to discredit me and laugh it off while the other two men are almost on the floor gasping for air at the hilarity of the moment.

"Oh I'm lying am I? Well I have camera's you didn't know about set up in my apartment, more specifically my bedroom. Proof is as easy as going to my car driving thirty minutes to my apartment and coming back with the evidence." I fold my arms across my chest and wait for his smart ass to test me. Truth was there were no tapes, but he didn't know that. When he gets quiet and looks down at his feet, I realize I'd won. "I thought so." I suck my teeth and march out of the mailroom.

I call the elevator and get on to go look for Jasmine on another floor. To my dismay, when the elevator doors open, Jane from accounting is standing in the elevator. "Ugh never mind, if you just left from seeing him, I don't want to see him anymore." Jane pretends to gag. "I thought he was done messing with your fat ass."

"First of all BITCH..." I begin to lay down the law on her ass, Jane is caught by surprise, I usually never go from zero to a hundred that quickly but the trials of the day have been piling up and getting on my nerves. "I ALREADY FUCKED THAT MAN, ENJOY MY SECONDS! You can have him! I don't want to deal with him or his attitude anymore! So spare me with that dumb shit." I get all in her face before finally pushing the 2nd floor button; Jasmine might be at Human Recourses; I know she has a lot of paperwork to fill in; she's still a fairly new employee. Jane presses the 3rd floor and stays quiet, pressing her body in a corner. Poor girl was probably terrified, the last time I raised my voice at her like that was in the bathroom last year when all her girls were clowning me. The elevator doors open on the 2nd floor, "And by the way BITCH, you need to come up with a better insult than calling me fat, because as you can see, I'm only one size away from your ass now. I've lost 40lbs and EVEN YOU can't deny I look DAMN good." I giggle at myself as I exit the lift leaving the frightened blonde girl, quiet and sick faced.

After not finding Jasmine on the entire 2nd floor with HR, I decide to go back to the fifth floor and just do the damn refiling myself. For all I knew she is probably faced down in a stall puking her brains out, after all, last night *was* very eventful.

When I arrive back on my floor from my fruitless wild goose chase, Evica is again at my desk stink faced. "Look I need my damn files organized and I told you that, WHERE THE HELL HAVE YOU BEEN?" This is the third battle I'm going to fight and it isn't even noon yet. "Look I don't care if you both want to waltz around the building adding numbers to your body counts, but this is an office building and we are here to wor---"

"FUCK YOU ERICA!" I scream at the top of my lungs before she can even finish her sentence. I intentionally call her by her birth name. My built up frustration has just hit a point of no return and I am ready to explode. "YOU HAVE NO FUCKING RIGHT TO TALK TO ME THE WAY YOU DO, KNOWING DAMN WELL I DO A SHIT LOAD OF WORK AROUND HERE! NOT TO MENTION I'VE SAVED YOUR COUSINS ASS FOR THE PAST THREE YEARS! YOU OWE ME A THANK YOU, NOT ALL THIS DISRESPECT!" And with that I begin making my way to Hogan's office to vent about the various attacks I've been enduring since I've walked into the office.

When I get to the beautifully carved wooden door, I am so angry I forget to knock. I barge in unannounced and find Jasmine on Bill's lap bouncing up and down on his dick. They don't even realize I'm in the room and keep going for a little while longer until I finally say, "Well there you are, you slut!" Hogan quickly pushes Jasmine off of him, and she scurries for her clothes which are laid out all across his office.

"FUCK BOTH OF Y'ALL! I QUIT!" I yell at them before storming out of Hogan's office. I bump into Evica and half the office outside of Bill's office. Everyone is looking in as he hurriedly zips up his pants, Jasmine is still topless. "I quit, I quit, I QUIT." I sing while making my way to my desk. Once I get to my seat I pack up all my shit; pictures of Jeremy and I, some personal files, my purse, everything within arm's reach... Then I head for the elevator.

The drive back to my apartment complex is somber except for the buzzing of my phone. I have missed calls from Evica, Jasmine, Greg, and William Hogan himself. I am so close to throwing my phone outside my car window, but I am able to contain myself. I'm surprised I'm not crying; it actually feels like a heavy weight has been lifted from my shoulders. I didn't have a game plan for how I was going to earn a pay check from here on out, but for the first time in a long time I feel completely care free and relaxed. I just hope I made the right decision.

Chapter 17: Gone

~2000 Present Day~

As soon as I unlock the door and enter into my apartment, I lose it. What the fuck did I just do? Tears start streaming down my face. I just quit a job where I made eighty-five thousand dollars a year, with no back up plan, and no college education; I am screwed. I fall to the floor and begin weeping, I hated my job so much and burned so many bridges in one day it wouldn't even feel right to go back with my tail in between my legs and beg for another chance. I saw how quickly Hogan replaced Louisa; I bet my replacement was already on their way. I have way too much pride to go back, and I really do hate everyone there.

Jeremy comes out from the bedroom when he hears me crying. "Baby?" I hear him walking slowly towards me, when he turns the corner I see he is holding a baseball bat. "God, you scared me... Why are you home so early? And oh my God, are you crying?" He hurries towards me and closes the front door. He picks me up and carries me to our bedroom. When he lays me on the bed and wipes away my tears he tucks me into the covers, makes sure I'm comfortable and waits until I calm down before asking me again to break down what was wrong.

"I quit my job." I say sobbing. "I can't stand it there, I've made way too many enemies, and it's really not worth the money. I am so sorry; I don't even know what I'm going to do now. I know we were trying to buy a house and everything, but now we might not be able to afford it." I cannot contain myself.

"Do you believe in God?" His response to my explanation is so random. I knew Jeremy was a spiritual, God-fearing man, but we had never really talked about it or attended church together in the past, so this was awkward for me.

"Yea... I mean, my mom is Christian, why?"

"I've been feeling him working in me lately baby, like... I don't trip over stuff like losing a job or quitting a job

140

because I finally realize all things work in His favor. You have to know there's a bigger picture."

"What are you even talking about?" I look at him crazy, he is kind of scaring me.

"Well, you are staring at the official music director for the new Tooley TXA Radio Station." He says with the biggest grin. "That's what I was trying to tell you. God is so good, when one door closes, another even bigger one opens. The offer they made me is big enough to support the both of us, have you go back to school and study what you really want to do, and we can still afford the house." He continues.

"OH MY GOODNESS BABY! I'M SO HAPPY FOR YOU!" I stand up on the bed and begin jumping up and down around him. "I CAN'T BELIEVE THIS!"

"I know, that's exactly how I felt. Before I got to Chicago I prayed about everything and just asked God to really guide the both of our futures and paths. I found out a few hours ago I officially got the job and just came back from the grocery store. I went to go buy some lobster with some other fancy things to cook and surprise you with for when you got home later today. You coming home now is a sign... That firm isn't where you belong. You always used to tell me about your love for writing, well... Now you can go back to school and actually be a writer." He is smiling so hard I can't help but kiss him.

"I don't know what I would do without you." I give him a tight embrace.

"Oh, you'd be fine without me; God is the one neither of us could live without." He kisses me on my forehead after I plop into his lap. We sit there for about an hour, talking about what our lives will be like with this new salary of his, which is almost double mine. He tells me he still wants to have his own business on the side, but that Monday through Friday he would be at the station. I realize the more Jeremy talks; the more I am completely captivated by him. I feel so bad for everything I have ever done behind his back and I begin to cry again. "What's wrong?" He asks, did I say something wrong. I shake my head no, "You're not crying about your job are

141

you?"

"No, no… I just have an amazing man, that's all. I don't need anyone else. I have you, I have my mom, and I have God. That's all I need. I realize that now." As soon as those words leave my lips I feel a sense of calm and understanding. "Can you pray for us?" I ask him, "Pray that God forgives me." He nods and begins to pray.

"Heavenly father, we thank You. Thank You for everything You are doing in the lives of my beautiful fiancé and I. I pray that You continue to order our steps from this point on, and that everything that is meant to happen will happen according to Your will. We thank You for everything You've done in our lives so far and we praise You in advance for everything You are about to do in our futures. Father God, even if You don't do one more thing in our lives we want to give You the highest praise and shout Hallelujah to the heavens just because of who You are. I pray for my new job with TXA and that You give me the drive to work hard and be an example of You in my new work environment. I also pray for the chapter You've closed in the life of my fiancé, Britney Greene. Father, I pray that You let her know that even though one door closes as long as she seeks Your Kingdom first, everything she could ever need and want will follow. I pray that You forgive any sins we have between the both of us, and that at this very moment You give us a fresh start as we start a new journey where we completely live for You. I pray all this, in the name of the one who saves; and together we say his name…"

"Jesus… Amen." We say in unison. The prayer was exactly what I needed, I truly feel delivered from all my sins. I say another little prayer inside of my head asking Jesus to come take over my life and I quietly accept him as my Lord and savior. Jeremy kisses my forehead and tells me he's going to head to the kitchen and begin preparing the lobster. When he gets up I turn on my side and smile, I really am a lucky girl.

I am close to falling asleep when my phone rings; it's Jasmine. I've been ignoring her calls all morning, I figured now that I'm in a better space I should answer my phone.

"Hello?" I finally say after taking a deep breath.

"Britney, I know you hate me, I don't know what to say other than I'm sorry."

"You're good. I don't hate anyone." I say verbally even though my tone says otherwise.

"I just want us to be friends again." She continues.

"Actually Jasmine… I forgive you but I don't know about us being friends."

"Why not?" I can hear her whimpering in the background. When I don't respond after a long pause, she continues talking. "I got suspended today... I think they're going to fire me; the whole office saw me naked. I never want to go back there."

"I mean… You did fuck Hogan in his office." I say matter-of-factly.

"And you fucked him in DC, what's the big deal?" I sense a little animosity in her tone. "Listen Brit, ever since we went to that concert you have treated me differently. I thought we told each other everything, we both admitted to doing some scandalous things in our lifetimes, so I don't know why you're judging me when your sins are just as stacked up as mine are." I can hear her start crying.

"Just because I have a past doesn't mean I'm trying to dwell in it. I haven't messed around in months and I made a decision to keep it that way." I start to whisper so Jeremy doesn't overhear my conversation. "I feel like I'm trying to change and you're still trying to be a ho." I think the word ho was the last straw for her.

"FUCK YOU MS. HOLIER THAN THOU! I HAVE BEEN NOTHING BUT NICE TO YOU AND YOU'RE TREATING ME LIKE A COMPLETE STRANGER! I was fucking molested as a child! I'm screwed up, and I admit that... okay? But I'm not about to sit here and let you judge me like you don't have dirt underneath your own damn fingernails. IF I'M A HO, YOU A HO TOO! Only difference between us is I'm not out here living a double life- *click*" I hang up on Jasmine before she can say another word. I was

143

done with her, she represented the old me and I was done with that lifestyle. I didn't mean to offend her but her behavior wasn't conducive to my character change. Honestly, I really don't even owe her an explanation, I told her what Hogan did to me and how miserable my life was at work ever since I got back from DC, and what does she do? Fuck Hogan anyways... In my eyes she was never really my *friend* to begin with. I start drifting off in my thoughts, until I finally fall sound asleep.

~Three Hours Later~

"WHAT THE FUCK IS THIS?" I wake up startled to my fiancé hovering over me with something gold in his hand.

"Huh? Baby what's wrong?" I say still trying to wipe the sleep from my eyes. I go white when I realize what's going on, Jeremy is standing over me holding an empty condom wrapper, "Where'd you get that?" I try buying some time in order to think up an excuse. The truth is, I knew damn well where the hell he got that; somewhere in this room. Greg used a condom on me in this very room about a month ago, I have no idea how it got in Jeremy's possession.

"When you fell asleep I decided to clean up and when I lifted the damn rug to vacuum I found this fucking condom wrapper on the floor. Now how the fuck did it get in my bedroom. I know you know so don't even think about lying to me."

"Are you sure it's not ours?" I pretend to be puzzled.

"BRITNEY GREENE IF YOU DON'T FUCKING TELL ME THE TRUTH I'M GOING TO THROW YOU OUT OF THIS APARTMENT RIGHT NOW!" I am startled by how loud and angry Jeremy is, I have never seen him this angry, not even the night of our first fight when I came home late and extremely drunk. "You and I haven't had sex in a while and when we fucking do, we NEVER use condoms, WHO THE FUCK HAVE YOU HAD IN OUR BEDROOM." He barks. I become numb; of course this happens the moment I give my life to Christ, right? The devil is mocking me right now. All the things I've done behind Jeremy's back are now

144

about to surface. All I can do now is tell the truth, the whole truth, and nothing but the truth. This will surely go down as the worst day of my life, when I lose both my job and my fiancé within hours of each other.

I motion Jeremy to sit down next to me. I try to put my hand in his curly hair and touch him one last time before his perfect image of me is tarnished forever, but he swats my hand away. "Start fucking talking." His demeanor is ice cold, there's no going back after this.

"I brought a co-worker home when you were in Chicago." I blurt out. I swear my soul escaped my body the same time the words left my lips.

"YOU DID WHAT?" Tears start streaming down his face. I don't think I've ever seen him flat out cry. I start crying too, the fact that I'm hurting him is hurting me more.

"I brought home a co-worker." I meekly repeat.

"God help me." Jeremy gets up from the side of the bed and begins pacing the room. "Jesus help me, because if I wasn't a Christian I would have gone across your face with my fist." He says in somewhat of a psychotic trance.

"I'll tell you whatever, just ask me, I'll tell you. I'm dirty, I'm a ho. I've had this issue for years I was just too afraid to tell you." I cry. "Go ahead and hit me if it will make you feel better, please, just hit me."

"DON'T TEMPT ME WOMAN! SO HELP ME GOD, DON'T TEMPT ME! I ALMOST FUCKING MARRIED YOU!" He comes so close to me and screams in my face. "YOU THINK YOU'RE SLICK HUH? SITTING UP HERE WITH ME PLAYING HOUSE, PRAYING WITH ME, GETTING ME TO FUCKING ALMOST MARRY YOU AND YOU HAVE THE NERVE TO GO AND BRING HOGAN INTO MY HOME?" Jeremy's entire face is turning red.

"Calm down baby, please calm down." I shut my eyes a little afraid that at any moment Jeremy's clenched fist will make excruciating contact with my jaw. He has always been the meekest, humblest man I know. There has never been a violent bone in Jeremy's body, but I know at this very moment he is at his wits end. I can see his heart being snatched out of his chest right before my eyes. "It wasn't Hogan." I manage to let out.

"So you never fucked Hogan? He just gave you a fucking promotion and shit and you never fucked him?" He stops pacing and stares me dead in the eye waiting for my response.

"I did fuck him, in DC. Not here. I brought another co-worker here." I cry even harder.

"So let me get this straight," Jeremy begins to laugh hysterically, "you not only fucked your boss on a business trip when you distinctively told me you wouldn't but you had another sucker in my fucking bed?" I close my eyes and nod, bracing myself for the blow.

"WHAT ELSE?" He barks. I want the whole truth. "How many other guys?"

"About eight or nine." I say low under my breath.

"I CAN'T HEAR YOU!" He screams so close to my face I can feel his spit land on me.

"ABOUT EIGHT OR NINE!" I cry back. "I fuck a lot of guys; I take them to the Vacation Inn. I have a problem and I never meant to hurt you... I like attention... I am so sorry..."

"Do I need to get fucking tested?" That was a good question; I hadn't been tested in a while either, so I nod.

"Why, you got some shit?" At this point Jeremy is talking to me like a stranger he picked up on the streets and I can't really blame him.

"I don't know; I don't think so... I used protection, but just to be safe, get tested." I honestly divulge.

"Lucky for you it's only 3PM and clinics are still open, I am going to get tested right now and by the time I come back, I want you out of this apartment." He grabs his keys and his wallet.

"JEREMY, PLEASE DON'T LEAVE ME." I run and cry after him. Jeremy stops at the door then turns to me.

"I loved you, you lying piece of shit. I loved you, and this is how you repay me? I did everything under the sun for you! I SEE HOW YOU LOOK AT OTHER MEN FROM

THE CORNER OF YOUR EYE. YOU THINK I DON'T
WANT TO FUCK OTHER BITCHES TOO? DON'T YOU
THINK I COULD BRING HOME MY OWN CO-
WORKERS? I am surrounded by millions of horny
bridesmaids a year who throw themselves at me almost the
same way you threw yourself at me when we first me. BUT
YOU KNOW WHAT, I DON'T GIVE IN! I have NEVER
fucking cheated on you Britney! Do you know why? ASK
ME WHY." He is livid.

"Why?" It takes all of the energy left in me to let out
that one word.

"BECAUSE I LOVED YOU BRITNEY! AND YOU
WERE ENOUGH FOR ME…" He cries louder that I've ever
heard another human being cry. "I JUST WANTED TO BE
ENOUGH FOR YOU, BRITNEY! But I guess I wasn't." I
lean in to wipe away his tears when he violently pushes my
hand away. "BE OUT BY THE TIME I COME BACK
FROM THE CLINIC WOMAN, OR SO HELP ME GOD I
AM NOT RESPONSIBLE FOR MY ACTIONS." And just
like that, Jeremy storms out of our apartment slamming the
door hard and finally leaves me… and our relationship.

I quickly run for my phone with the idea of calling
him and begging for forgiveness, but I know it will only make
him angrier and I figure he needs his space. Plus, I have no
idea what I would even say to him if he gave me the floor to
speak. I never deserved him; I might as well just let him go
find happiness with a better woman. "He's gone." I say under
my breath as I retreat back to the bedroom. I sit emotionlessly
on the corner of my bed staring at my phone. I have a lot of
missed calls but only two voicemails. I muster up the courage
to listen to them; I mean my life is already in shambles,
what's the point of hiding from even more bad news? *Bring it
on!* I think to myself while dialing "1".

The first message is from Hogan: *"Britney, this is
William. If I don't hear from you in the next five minutes I'm
going to assume you abandoned ship like Louisa, and you'll
never be able to come back and work for my firm again.
click"

The second message is also from Hogan, this time he is screaming into the phone and there is a lot of anger in his tone: *"BRITNEY, DAMNIT! YOU HAD SO MUCH POTENTIAL AND YOU'RE GOING TO THROW IT ALL AWAY BECAUSE YOU WALKED IN ON JASMINE AND I? THAT'S CHILDISH. LISTEN, YOU SAW HOW QUICKLY I REPLACED LOUISA? WELL WITH HOW MUCH YOUR POSITION PAYS, YOUR REPLACEMENT WILL BE EVEN EASIER TO FIND. EVERYONE IS REPLACEABLE BRITNEY, REMEMBER THAT. AND IF I DON'T HEAR FROM YOU IT'LL BE YOUR LOSS! *click*"*

I worked my butt off for that firm, I know the only reason Bill is this angry with me is because without me, his job becomes ten times harder. I delete both messages and get up to begin packing all of my stuff. I have a feeling Jeremy wasn't bluffing about me getting the fuck out of the apartment, and I wasn't about to stick around and find out what would happen if he came back home and found I was still here.

I reach for suitcases which are kept in the highest part of our closet and a little box falls on my foot... It's a ring box... a *hidden* ring box. I pick it up and take a deep breath before opening it. It's a beautiful, three-stone, diamond engagement ring. I figure out that Jeremy might have wanted to propose to me today after the lobster dinner he planned on preparing. I can't believe everything went south in just a matter of hours. I put the ring back up where it fell from and continued to pack my things... I have *REALLY* fucked up; my heart is gone.

Chapter 18: What Doesn't Kill You...

~2000 Present Day~

[*Dear Jeremy, I wish you were my first...*] I put the pen down and begin to cry. I can't even get myself to write him a letter without completely losing it emotionally. I've been a wreck for the past five days. In the past week, I've moved all my belongings in to my mother's house in Dumois. The most awkward part about the whole move was seeing Jenna Jackson again (my mother's neighbor who hates me). She sat outside on her lawn giving me a death stare as I moved in my luggage. I wouldn't be surprised if my mother told her my situation, I think they've rekindled their relationship. By now Mrs. Jackson is probably convinced I am the devil, sent here to ruin lives one sexual encounter at a time. I haven't asked my mother about the whereabouts of Jenna's ex-husband Deon, for all I know they could have gotten back together; fortunately for the past five days I haven't seen him.

Living back in Dumois is humbling, the mice and roaches, the old furniture, the bathroom mold... Now I really regret quitting my job because I could have used that money to help my mother get out of this place a lot sooner, unfortunately for me I was being selfish and left because I was emotionally drained. Being 27 has brought on nothing but heartache and pain. I lost my job, my first female friend, I moved back to Dumois, *and* my fiancé left me... What other traumatic experiences do I have to look forward to?

I wipe my tears and decide to throw away the one-line letter I had started. I crumple the piece of paper and shoot it into a pink bin beside me. I can't believe my room still looks the exact same way I left it four years ago. You'd think Mama Emma would have thrown out all my shit and turned it into whatever she wanted, but she left everything as is. I found a lot of my old journals in here too. Damn, I used to write A LOT. Stories, scripts, etc.... I've had this same room since elementary school so I even found coloring books where I turn the pictures into full blown children's stories. I'd hand write my own words underneath each picture. I'd color in and write "by Britney Greene" on the cover page with a permanent marker. I really miss those simple, happy days.

"BRITNEY!" I hear my mom calling from down stairs. "DINNER'S READY!" She didn't have to tell me twice. I speed down the squeaky, dusty, wooden staircase and make my way to the kitchen. I smell crawfish soup. God, I forgot how much I missed my mother's cooking. Every night since I've been here I've been in heaven. She fixes me a bowl and as I'm about to turn and take it upstairs to my room, like I'd been doing for the past couple of days she stops me. "Now young lady, I've given you your space and time to grieve but I really think tonight we need to talk."

"Uh… Mom, I don't feel like talking." I sigh.

"I know you hate the sound of my voice, but we need to talk about what's next in your life. You don't have a job anymore nor do you have a plan, and I'll be damned if I allow you to move backwards in life after accomplishing so much. Now I cooked you a great meal, and I'm letting you stay here for free, the least you can do is eat dinner with me." My old lady was right, surprisingly since I've moved in she's let me grieve in peace, I've spent five days straight in my room. I haven't even showered, I'm a mess and I am completely lost when it comes to what to do next.

"Okay." I surrender. After she fixes her own bowl we

make our way to the dining room table and we sit. As I'm about to dive into my food my mother grabs my hand, suggesting we pray. I submissively put down my spoon and bow my head. The last time I prayed was with Jeremy, so naturally tears began to stream down my face. I quietly use my other had to wipe them away. I didn't want her to see me crying.

"Dear Father God, Thank You for bringing my daughter and I together again, please bless this food and as we partake in it, let You instill in us humility and gratefulness, because no matter what we think we're going through, there is always someone out there in Your big beautiful world going through much worse. I pray for Britney's ability to heal and to move forward in her life and still continue to be successful, I pray against any strongholds that have a grip on her life preventing her from using her sexuality in the way You'd like her to. Father God, I love my daughter, so I know You love her way more than I could ever fathom. Please let Your will be done in our lives. In the name of Jesus, I pray, Amen."

"Amen." I respond to the prayer. I still don't know how I feel about religion. The same day I officially made the decision to give my life to Christ my whole world fell apart… Jesus and I aren't on the best of terms. I'm beginning to question everything about what I was raised to believe. I remember how great life was in the weeks that I believed I was in control of my own destiny. I start to contemplate dabbling in witchcraft as we begin eating, maybe it'll help me get Jeremy back. The thought escapes my head as soon as it enters it, probably due to the food being so amazing. My taste buds are doing somersaults; there is no cooking that tastes as good as Mama Emma Greene's cooking. As I take the last sip of my crawfish soup I look up to find my mother staring straight at me. I take a deep breath and proceed to slowly put my spoon down… Here comes the long avoided talk.

"Did I ever tell you the story of how your father and I met?" My mother's face lights up as she speaks.

"No." I giggle, my mother rarely ever spoke about my father unless she was cursing me out and letting me know I was behaving exactly like he used to, plus I stopped seeing him when I was around six years old, even though he didn't actually die until I was twelve. So any bits of his life story I could get out of her felt like Christmas.

"Jordan Greene was my first lust..." She began.

"Lust?" I laugh. "Not love?"

"I meant what I said, now do you want me to finish this story or not?" My mother says sternly, although I continue to laugh.

"Go 'head Momma." I chuckle.

"Like I was saying, Jordan Greene was my first Lust. He was so handsome and cool.
Here in Dumois he was what you young girls call 'the shit'. He had tattoos, he smoked cigarettes, he drove a motorcycle, he played the guitar, all the girls wanted him… And of course, so did I." I could see the sparks in my mother's eyes as she reminisced. "I was only seventeen when I met him, the dilemma was; I had a boyfriend at the time. His name was Willie and he was just as country as they come. Willie was a good guy, hardworking but damn was he boring as hell. I wanted to get out of Dumois; I didn't want to stay here my whole life. One of the things most appealing about your father was he told me about all the places he would take me if I was his girl. We even talked about going to Africa on our honeymoon. See your father was a big sweet talker. He got me to leave my good boyfriend Willie for him." I start to think about my own past… about how I left David for Anthony. Was my father to Emma what Anthony Johnson is to me? The thought of that made me sad. At least I didn't get pregnant by my heartbreaker. "Willie was devastated when I left him," My mother sadly recalls. "Last I heard, he got a job at the post office and was able to apply for a position out of state, so maybe if I stuck with him and kept my head out of the clouds, I'd be out of Dumois as well… But I made the reckless decision to be with your father. I got pregnant young so my father forced Jordan to marry me even though your grandfather never liked him. Jordan hated me for tying him down. The first six years of your life I raised you as a single

153

parent while your father ran the streets with these women. He never got a job which forced me to be on welfare and live in public housing. I didn't want to get a divorce, I never believed in it, but the government would give me more benefits as a legally single woman, so I had no choice but to leave your father. I still would let him sweet talk his way into my bed some nights because he fed me promises of getting back together and taking us away. All I wanted was a stable family for you; maybe you would have turned out differently when it comes to the way you interact with men." She begins to cry.

"Momma, please don't cry." I start sobbing as well. "You did the best you could do, the issues have to do with me, and not anything you did."

"I can't help but feel like I wronged you." She gets a tissue and blows her nose, and hands me one too before continuing her story. "Anyways, one night your daddy came over when you were asleep and began to violently shiver after we had sex. I woke him up but he wouldn't stop shaking. I called an ambulance and they took him to the hospital. I didn't want to wake you up because you were fast asleep and I didn't want you to see that he and I were still seeing each other. Later the doctor called me and told me your daddy had AIDs. The doctor suggested I come up to the hospital as soon as possible and get myself tested. I dropped to my knees and cried out to the heavens." She starts shaking while recalling the horrific night.

"I think I remember your screams that night... I was like ten years old." Back then I had no idea those screams had anything to do with my father's illness. I just remember hearing my mother shouting one night and I chucked it up to her screaming from a broken heart. After my father and her divorced when I was six, she'd always cry late at night. The only difference is, on that particular night, her screams were even more heart shattering. "I came out to check on you, and you told me you were fine and to go back to sleep. I had no idea you were going through so much."

"You were only ten." Tears stream down her face. "How do you tell a ten-year-old both her parents might have

AIDs and are dying? Anyways, while you were at school the next day I went up to the hospital. While I was waiting for the results your father tried to talk to me and feed me dreams. I remember him saying 'I'm sorry Emma; if we both got it now then we can be together and live out the rest of our lives together." It was like he knew he had it all along and was trying to get me to die with him. I didn't say a word to him that day; in my mind he was already dead. When the doctor came back with my results, they were negative. I couldn't believe it. Neither could your father, he looked defeated. The man tried to bring me down, he tried to kill me... but thanks to God I survived. I got on my knees in the hospital that day and gave my life to Christ. I have never had sex since that night. I have dedicated my entire life to raising you and trying my best to raise you right, but when you turned nineteen, I started seeing you behave more like your father."

"I know," I sigh. "But honestly I think I actually started acting more like you, because I left my good, hard-working high school boyfriend for Anthony Johnson. A boy I lusted for who didn't love me. Momma that boy Anthony broke me just like daddy broke you." I start to whale. "I have no self-esteem or self-worth because of him. I was so hurt when he left that's why I started acting reckless and having sex with so many different men, including Mr. Jackson. I don't know why I let a man make me so weak, Momma. I HATE myself and what I've done to people, but I swear I had prayed about it and was going to change my life. I stopped having sex months ago, and then Jeremy randomly found evidence of that last time I cheated. Now he's gone and my life is ruined." I can't breathe, I'm crying so hard. My mother leans in closer to me and cradles my head in her arms.

"Shh baby, don't cry, Britney. I'm glad I heard you say you prayed on it and recognized your wrong."

"But Momma, I don't know if I can believe in anything anymore... especially not Jesus. I feel broken." I inform her.

"Baby I can't force you to believe what I believe; all I know is what I've experienced. And I can only pray that one-day God opens the eyes of your heart as well. Jeremy is a good man but I promise if you get on and stay on a righteous path you'll find yourself someone just as good as he was. You just have to stay and be faithful."

"Momma, I don't want anyone else." I say exasperated. "I just want Jeremy."

"I know baby. Just know there are two kinds of men in this world, the good ones and the ones that will rot your heart, body, mind, and soul if you let them. Live for Christ and stop having sex, even if you think you've found "the one". That's how you find a good man. The only man for me is Jesus, but you... you're still young and need to have your own child one day so you can't give up. Just promise me you won't be out here having no more sex until you get married one day."

"I promise." I say reluctantly as I feel my tears wetting up her blouse.

"Good girl." She cradles me for about half an hour until we both stop crying.

"You're so right Momma; I'm done with men with bad intentions. I'm going to focus on getting you and me out of Dumois. I'm going to make you proud again, you'll see." I smile at her and she smiles back at me with her puffy eyes.

"Have you thought about a plan?" She probes.

"Well for starters, I'm going to sell my car and all those fancy clothes I have in those suitcases upstairs. That should give us enough money to last almost a year. I'm also going to use some of that money to go back to Tooley Community College."

"What do you want to major in?" She asks, smiling hard, obviously proud of my decision making.

"I don't know... Writing? English? I want to teach or do something in journalism." I share.

"Wow, I didn't know you still loved to write." She laughs. "You used to write me some of the most beautiful poems for Mother's Day... I still have every single one."

"Yea Momma, I still love to write. I only wanted to work for Hogan & Wildes because I wanted the notoriety.

156

Truth is, law firms are boring as hell to me and far from my passion. Working there was miserable and unfulfilling." I admit.

"Well, all that sounds like a great plan. How about you worry about men after you graduate, you'll be twenty-nine by then, perfect age to find a good husband and settle down."

"You're right Momma." I laugh, "for the next two years; all I'm going to focus on is my plan."

"Good girl!" She cheers me on.

"Well Momma, this was an AMAZING talk but it's been emotionally draining and I think we both need our rest. I think I'm going to head upstairs now and go to bed" We both get up from our chairs and I give her a big embrace. "By the way, thank you for sharing your story Momma, I am so proud of you. You did a lot, and your God kept you here, disease free, for a reason. We're going to make it out of Dumois together! In life we fall down, but we get back up."

"He's your God too, just wait you'll see… and thank you, I receive it in the name of Jesus." My mother chants as she begins making her way up the steps humming an old gospel song.

"Amen." I subconsciously say under my breath as I clear the table. After I wash the dishes I head to my own room for the night. I sit at my little desk and attempt to write to Jeremy one last time:

[*Dear Jeremy, I wish you were my first… I wish I wasn't so fucked up. I wish I made a decision to change my life a lot earlier. I wish I had my shit together before I met you. You don't deserve the pain I put you through. You have been nothing but beautiful, hard-working, and faithful. I've cheated on you, I've lied to you, I've taken you for granted, and I wish I had an excuse for why I did the things I did, but I don't. I've tried to call you for the past five days since I've moved in with my mom but I understand you don't want to hear from me. I am a heartless person, I don't have any emotions, and I am cold like ice… But being by your side was the only thing that humanized me. I miss your touch, your* smell, and your smile, but most of all I miss being loved, because honestly besides my mother… You're all I've got… Or better yet you're all I had. So now I feel lonelier than lonely, and I have no one to blame but myself. You were the only glimpse of true love I've ever known and I took you for granted. I honestly don't remember the names of all the men I slept with in my lifetime, I don't know why I kept doing it, I just know that the first time I got my heart broken stuck with me my entire life. That's why I say I wish you were my first. I probably wouldn't have turned out so fucked up. I am a bitter, jealous, angry, evil being. I don't know why I'm the way I am, I just am. I grew up poor and fatherless, I've been used by countless men, and I just don't have my emotions in check. I don't know why I'm writing you this like you'd ever give me another chance, but I just wanted you to know what I was thinking about you. I had made up my mind to clean up my life and stop cheating about a month before you found that condom wrapper. In fact, the night I had sex with that co-worker was the last time I cheated on you. I realized no man could be as beautiful inside and out as you are. I realized I needed to stop taking you for granted and reciprocate the love I got from you. I swear on my father's grave I was really trying, but I guess the universe wanted me to reap what I sowed and things happened the way they did. I will take this as a learning experience. I also wanted to tell you that I found the ring…. The ring I think you were going to give me that night. I guess your God answered your prayers and showed you how I've really been treating you before you had the chance to slip that ring on my finger, huh? All I can say is I am truly sorry, and if given another chance, I promise to never hurt you again, I promise to dedicate my whole life to making you smile and being your backbone. If we are meant to be I hope that you find your way back into my arms so I can have another chance to treat you the way you deserve to be treated. That's all for now, please write back… Love, Britney.]

The next day I take my letter to the post office and mail it out.

Chapter 19: Class is in Session

~2001 Present Day~

It is my first day of school and I am sitting in my first class of the day in utter disbelief. If you would have told me four months ago, around the time I turned twenty-seven, that I would be enrolled in Tooley Community College full time, in hopes of attaining an associate's degree in communications (with a focus in Journalism), I would have thought you were crazy. As a matter of fact, a lot about my life has changed in such a short period of time, I hardly recognize myself. For one, I no longer have a job, which isn't necessarily a bad thing considering my disdain for where I used to work, and two, I have been living back at home in Dumois with my mother for several months now. Spending the holidays in the home I grew up in with my mother was refreshing.

In order to be sitting in this class, I have had to make a lot of sacrifices such as, selling my Mercedes as well as a lot of my high end clothing. I have to be honest, it was heartbreaking having to part with all my tailored Louie Verdone suits, but it was the only way I was going to be able to pay for my education without having to get a job. I am hoping that obtaining this degree and furthering my education is what will catapult me back into being financially stable. It might take me a while to make the amount of money I once made at the law firm, but at least I'll finally be doing something I'm passionate about. Right now I may be down, but I have way too much ambition to be out.

Luckily for me, when I attended the Annual Business Gala in DC, Jeremy wasn't the only one who benefited occupationally. While networking at the event, I also exchanged contact information with the president and owner of The AJMC (American Journalism and Media Company), Dan Marshall. Miraculously, the new local paper printed here in Tooley, which has only been in business for the past year, is published by the AJMC. I must have made a positive and lasting impression on Mr. Marshall at the gala, because after sending in samples of my writing, and communicating my interest in working for The Tooley Times, I was promised a mid-entry position upon the completion of a two-year degree.

Working for The Tooley Times would be an amazing job for me, regardless of them being a fairly new paper. The organization already has some acclaimed journalists on board and their subscriptions are growing immensely. Writing is my passion so I intend to work hard in school and not divert from the plan.

"Good morning class, I am Professor Tara Allen… Welcome to English 101." I can't stop smiling. I watch from the very back of the class while all the other students get settled into their seats. There is a young man sitting to my right whose gaze I periodically feel on my person, but I have zero interest in entertaining his subtle advances. Don't get me wrong, a year ago I would have already slipped him a note with my number on it and made plans to meet up with him at the Vacation Inn after class, but unfortunately for him; today, I am a new and improved woman. The kid can't be a day over twenty-three and he has that 'preppy, college boy' image going for him. Come to think of it, he is actually *extremely* sexy… But I'm still not biting, I am solely here to acquire an education; I don't allow myself to even look in his direction.

"Hey, psst." I hear him whisper. "Nice watch! What is

that… a Rolex?" I nod without even bothering to look up at him. I decided to keep the Rolex watch I had bought for Greg; there was no way I would ever give Jeremy a rejected gift intended for a man I was cheating on him with. I got my own name engraved over Greg's followed by the phrase *'Live and Learn'*. I didn't care that it was a man's watch, wearing it made me feel powerful. It is probably the only luxury item I have left that I bought with my Hogan & Wildes salary that I didn't end up pawning.

"How much was it? If it's real, it's got to be about eight grand." He says inspecting my wrist.

"I don't know; it was a gift." I lie trying my best to be as short as possible. I am really trying to pay attention to the professor. Preppy boy finally gets the hint and leaves me alone. An hour later, a tall, skinny, blonde girl walks through the doors and is speaking loudly into her cell phone.

"Nice of you to join us." Professor Allen sarcastically calls out to the girl who is so distracted by her conversation that she doesn't even hear the remark. The blonde girl is being very inconsiderate and she doesn't seem to care. At this point the entire class stops focusing on the professor all together and is staring at the loud blonde and giggling. I overhear colloquial "California valley girl" from pieces of her phone conversation as she takes a seat in the row directly in front of me. She must be one of many out-of-towners that have migrated to our newly gentrified city in the past couple of years. Even though she's distracting and annoying I am somewhat grateful for her appearance because Mr. Young Preppy Boy to my right is now focused solely on her. "Excuse me?" Professor Allen finally decides to confront the girl after the disruption becomes unbearable.

"Yea… Jocelyn, like, I'm going to have to call you back. Like, my professor is so focused on what I'm doing instead of teaching this class…. Like, I know right… I'll call you after class… Okay… Okay… Smooches back at ya!" The whole class looks on as the girl finally hangs up her phone. I guess since it is the first day of class the Professor lets the ignorant behavior slide and just continues teaching the class as if nothing happened.

A couple of minutes later when eyes were no longer on the back of the class, the preppy boy sitting to my right suddenly hops over the aisle into a seat right next to the disruptive girl. He is extremely bold for first day etiquette; I can't tell anymore how old he is. I get the feeling now that he's probably fresh out of high school and can't wait to plow down his first college girl. That's the only way I can explain his eagerness. He was probably the man in his high school and judging by his toned body, he was probably a star athlete. I bet he could have made it into a better school if he focused less on girls and more on his grades. All this is speculation of course, but lately I've been a good judge of character.

"What's up?" I hear him say to the blonde.

"Hi." She smiles at him. I can't tell if that's an 'I'm interested' smile or a 'not in this life time, buddy' smile; whichever one it is she obviously has him wrapped around her pretty little manicured finger.

"I was watching you while you came in, you look really good." He says with the confidence of a man who's never been turned down in his life.

"Thanks." The blonde giggles, I guess it was an 'I'm interested' smile after all. Then again, who wouldn't be interested in this tall, dark, and handsome, in shape, preppy boy with a contagious smile?

"I'm Anthony, and you are?" He says to her, as I nearly choke on my spit. Oh God, OF COURSE his name is *Anthony*. That right there is a sign from God to stop eavesdropping and just focus on my professor. I swear every villainous male must be named Anthony. I bet this Anthony treats women just like Anthony Johnson does. His name is a major turn off so I remove myself from the rest of their flirty conversation and begin to focus all my attention on the lesson.

Twenty minutes later Professor Allan finally dismisses the class and I am thankful. I haven't been in a classroom for over nine years; I knew this two hour and a half English 101 course was going to be problematic... At least I didn't fall asleep.

"… Anyways I might not be at school for too long. I like, just got a call back from that Hogan & Wildes law firm this morning, and like, with what they offered to pay me, like, who fucking needs school?" The blonde girl says, snapping me back into their conversation.

"That's a HUGE deal, girl! Shit, if I got a job at that firm I wouldn't be here either. I heard even the mail clerks and cleaning crew get *paid.* I've been applying there since I was sixteen with no luck. I heard Will Hogan doesn't hire young, good looking guys like me and all the other male lawyers are ugly and old." He bursts out laughing. If only he knew how close to the truth, he was. That's why there was such chatter when Greg got hired; he was probably the first good looking, young man Hogan has ever accepted.

"Oh well give me your number, once I get on the inside I'll see what I can do." She smiles as she hands him her cell phone.

"So what are you going to be doing there?" He asks as he stores in his contact information and hands her back her cell.

"I'm going to be a lead legal secretary. I met Bill while I was bartending at a club last month and he told me to apply. I thought he was lying about who he said he was because we get a lot of 'drunk, dream sellers' at the bar, but when I went to the interview, sure enough, like, it was legit." She giggles. Damn, I guess Hogan was being honest when he said *everyone* is replaceable… this girl must be my replacement.

"That's what's up! Sounds dope." Preppy Anthony says.

"EXTREMELY DOPE! I'll be making like eighty thousand dollars a year *and* I'll be working directly for Hogan."

"Do you already have a degree or something?" He inquires.

"No, none at all, I just got my GED recently. I told Bill all of this and he didn't even care. He was drunk and flirting with me the whole time we spoke. I didn't even really

163

get interviewed. I just called the number he gave me and spoke directly to the Human Resources manager, and like they took down my information and told me to come in the next day for fingerprinting." She sings. I can't believe how reckless the law firm I once revered is now being with their new hires. Years ago when I first applied people took working there seriously, now it seems Hogan is randomly picking pretty women off the streets to work for *and under* him.

"DAMN, I'm still stuck on the salary." Anthony chuckles.

"I know right! And I might be going to DC in couple of months for that gala that's always in the news. I heard Bill takes his secretaries every year so I'm assuming that means I'm going!" She brags.

"That's so dope, please, please; please make sure to put in a good word for me once you get settled in. My mother would freak out if I told her I got a job there. And if I got paid what you're about to, I would *definitely* quit school!" He howls.

"Yea... I swear, once I have it in writing and its official, you'll never see me again in this wacky ass school." I listen on in disbelief as I pack up my binder and make my way out of the classroom. I can't believe my replacement at the firm was sitting directly in front of me, what a small world. I take all this as a sign from God; I am where I need to be… in school. I can't help but to think I used to be as simple minded as that blonde girl; she has no idea what she is getting herself into when it comes to Hogan. I start feeling guilty for not jumping in the conversation and warning that poor woman. *Oh well... She's old enough to make her own decisions.* I think to myself as I walk towards the library to purchase the books I'll need for the rest of my classes.

~1997 Flashback~

I was only with the firm for about four months before I saw my first celebrity come through the building. I was downstairs in the lobby on my way out to lunch when I noticed a crowd of hundreds surrounding the building.

"What's going on?" I asked Don Bates, who was one of my many on looking co-workers.   "That's Cindy Simon." He said rolling his eyes.

"Who?" I asked feeling out of the loop.

"She's an up and coming singer…" I still looked lost so he continued, "She dated Homeboy Duggar for a while." Mr. Bates was one of the best criminal defense attorneys that Hogan & Wildes, LLP ever had. He had over thirty years of experience and it was kind of sad on my part that this man *in his sixties* knew more about pop culture than I did.

"I don't know who either of those people are." I laughed.

"Well they're famous as hell, and she's here to see Hogan." Don said sounding unenthused. "Mark my words; this firm is going to turn into a joke in a couple of years." He added unexpectedly.

"Why do you say that?" I asked.

"Keep your eyes peeled and your mouth shut. We're already the laughing stock of corporate America thanks to our phenomenal leader. Bill is *always* in the damn tabloids with his pants pulled down to his ankles. Now he's defending this pop star against her record label, knowing damn well he'll never win the case. He's just doing it for the attention, as if he doesn't get enough of that already as it is."

"Oh… But all those people seem to be her fans. Isn't this a good way to bring free publicity to the firm and making us some more money?" I asked naively.

"You're just a pion in this grand train wreck waiting to happen, be thankful and consider that a blessing. There is so much crookedness going on in this firm…" Mr. Bates stops himself mid-sentence. "I've already said too much… just trust me… go back to school, and find a better job somewhere else. This place is not all it's cracked up to be." He scoffed as we watched Cindy Simon's security rush her from her car to the building, weaving through the swarm of people.

"If you don't mind me asking sir, if this is such a bad place… why don't *you* leave?"

"I will." He replied while abruptly leaving me in the

lobby and following Cindy Simon's entourage towards the elevators. Don Bates put in his two weeks' notice days after that incident and is now a big time lawyer in New York. Unfortunately, back then I didn't take his advice because my better judgment was clouded by the glitz and glamor that came with working for one of the best law firms in the Midwest.

Chapter 20: Old Habits Must Die

~2001 Present Day~

I am awakened by my cell phone ringing non-stop; I squint at my alarm clock on the side table by my bed and see that it's only 3am. I am still too sleepy to reach for my phone which is on the same side table. Who the hell could be calling me this early when I have class in a couple of hours? Then suddenly I jump at the thought of the phone call being from Jeremy. Maybe he finally cooled off after marinating on the letter he received from me months back. I quickly reach for my phone and finally answer it.

"Hello?" I hold my breath. The number wasn't familiar, maybe Jeremy had gotten a new cell?

"Hey girl! Where the hell have you been? I've been trying to contact you for months!" The voice is familiar but I really can't place a finger on which person it belongs to... I just know it damn sure isn't Jeremy's, and I'm disappointed by that.

"Who's this?" I ask, annoyed that whoever it was got my hopes up and had my heart racing.

"Adam." The voice slurs.

"Adam?" I am racking my brain trying to figure out where I know that name from.

"... From Burger Royale!" He adds before I can figure it out on my own.

"Oh... *Adam*. Hey what's up? It's kind of early and I have to be up for class in a couple of hours." I sigh.

"Yea, yea whatever girl, I know you've been avoiding me. I had to call you from my friend's phone in order for you to pick up, huh? Also in the past when I've called you during regular business hours, you always say you're busy at work." He's right. I've been avoiding the hell out of him ever since he caused the first fight I ever had with Jeremy. I even blocked his cell number, I was getting calls from him at least twice a week and I didn't want any negative distractions in my life.

"Look..." I start to turn him down easy.

"Look nothing! I'm heading to the Vacation Inn right now, I know I've been an asshole and haven't been treating you right. I want to make it up to you tonight. I will buy the room and everything." He begins to barter.

"Adam, I'm just not in the same place I used to be emotionally. I don't want to keep living like this." I say exasperated.

"Girl, you and I have so much fun together, plus we're cut from the same damn freak flag. Once a freak, always a freak! Don't tell me you've gone all *good girl* and shit when you were just sucking my dick last year." He ignorantly laughs.

"Adam I'm going to go now. And I'm not claiming to be a *good girl*; I'm just saying I am no longer at a place in my life where I want to meet random men at 3am in hotel rooms. I want better for myself, and as amazing as the sex between us was, I'm still not trying to move backwards and do the same shit I used to do." I explain.

"Listen, I'm not trying to upset you or anything. All I'm saying is that people like you and I don't change. Like I said, once a freak, always a freak. Once a cheater, always a cheater! Those are straight FACTS! You might be sick of my dick or whatever, I don't care, but you'll just go and do what we did with a new guy. If you want to go ahead and raise your body count number, that's on you. If I was a girl, I would find that one side dude to constantly give it to you good and keep your fiancé as well. It doesn't look good for you to be hoping around to your fiancé, to me, and now to whomever else you might be fucking." I can hear the drunkenness in his voice. Who the hell did this man think he was giving me suggestions on how I should live my life as a woman? Last time I checked, my vagina belonged to me!

"This is the last thing I'm going to say to you before I wish you goodbye forever, Adam. I am no longer with my fiancé, so me trying to change has nothing to do with not wanting to cheat. I just don't want a hotel relationship and a life full of random escapades. I don't want to have any more 'no strings attached' relationships with you or anyone else for that matter. I want better for myself, and if you don't want better for yourself and aren't willing to discontinue bad habits, then you're wrong; you and I are nothing alike." I calmly explain. "So goodbye Adam, unfortunately, despite your beliefs, I am focusing on cleaning up my life and that includes changing a lot of things." And with that I hang up before he even gets a chance to respond. I make a mental note to change my number later in the day... If he doesn't believe I can change, I'll show him at least my number can.

I am exhausted in English class this morning but still really enjoy being here. It's literally the highlight of my week; I guess writing really is my passion. I am in good spirits because Professor Allen has just recognized me for writing one of the best essays that she claims she's ever read. The class gave me a standing ovation after she read an excerpt of my writing aloud. It was an opinion piece on the gentrification of our city. It only took me eight hours to do all the research and write fifteen pages.

There is only about a half hour left of class and a piece of everyone's essay had been read. "Okay guys, great job on that last project. Are you ready for your next one?" Professor Allen sings.

"Oh man!" The class collectively responds.

"Don't worry, it won't be as hard as that last essay, *and* this time I'll permit working in groups of two or three." She laughs at the miserable faces sitting in front of her. Tara Allen is an amazing teacher, by far my favorite professor this semester. I've only been in her class for a couple of months and I've already learned a lot. She has a low haircut and is a single woman in her mid-forties, I'm pretty sure she's a lesbian because all I ever see her in is pants, *but I could be wrong*. Only a few teachers in my lifetime have really encouraged my love for learning; Professor Allen is definitely one of them. We spoke for about an hour after she dismissed class last week, and I told her about my goal of landing a job with The Tooley Times. She had some very encouraging words for me that day and they helped motivate me into writing that last essay she praised.

"As long as I get to work with the beautiful Britney Greene then I'm down." I am snapped out of my thoughts because Anthony (the preppy boy in my class) is standing up being his usual 'class clown' self, professing his 'lust' for me. The class erupts in laughter after his statement. He is so embarrassing and always has something mischievous to say. The *old* me would have found this very flattering, but since I'm not new to the game of lust, I understand he is just a player playing a game. I literally sat behind him for weeks watching him attempt to get the blonde girl to go out with him, but ever since she dropped out of school and went to replace me at Hogan & Wildes, I've been the focus of his attention in class. Unfortunately for him, I am not at all interested.

"Okay class calm down." Professor Allen laughs off Anthony's comment. "… And Anthony, maybe it'll be a good thing if Britney agrees to work with you. I mean, if you're lucky enough to have her as a partner maybe your grades will improve… Cause boy, are they struggling at the moment!" The class erupts in laughter again, except this time Anthony isn't laughing with them. When the next project is assigned and it is actually time to pick a group, Anthony begins to walk towards me. I roll my eyes already knowing where this is headed.

"So… You want to be partners?" He asks giving me a pearly white smile.

"I don't care, as long as you're serious. I'm really focused on my grades and I don't want you slacking off and having me work twice as hard." I honestly express.

"Got it!" He is visibly excited about my decision.

"And actually, since the project is due next week I wanted to get a start on it today. Do you mind meeting me at the library later tonight?" I ask as a way to test his motives; it is a Friday night; no *preppy jock* wants to spend their Friday nights researching for a paper.

"Okay…" He hesitantly agrees.

"Cool then, it's settled. See you at the library at

seven." Suddenly the class is dismissed and I hurriedly make my way to the bus stop. I have two errands to run before my math class at 4PM. I want to stop at my old apartments to finally check on Jeremy and then go get my phone number changed. Jeremy hasn't returned any of my calls and I haven't spoken to him since the day I moved out. I don't want too much time to pass between us before we speak because then I might never get a second chance. How is he able to go all these months without me? Doesn't he love me anymore? He hasn't even replied to my letter. I muster up the courage and make up my mind to go knock on the door of our old apartment and finally speak to him face to face. If he rejects me in person after several months of us not seeing each other, I'll know it's really over. I am hoping the sight of me rekindles our love and he embraces me as soon as he lays eyes on me.

The bus stops directly in front of the Tooley Towne Apartments. Even though I just recently moved out late last year, it feels like an eternity since I've been back here. My stomach is in knots as I exit the bus. Once at the door of the occupancy I once shared with Jeremy, I compose myself and take a deep breath before I finally knock. What seems like eternity goes by and still no one comes to the door. I have no idea what his new job schedule is like so I knock one more time... again, nothing. I press my ear to the door and it is quiet, I doubt he's ignoring me, I'm pretty sure no one is home. Although discouraged I decide to come back and try again after my meeting with Anthony-number-two at the library.

As I turn to leave one of my old neighbors opens up her apartment door. "Hey Mrs. Williams." I smile.

"Britney? My God, it's been a while. I kept asking Jeremy where you were and he said you moved back in with your mom. I didn't want to press the issue, but is everything okay?" She inquires while giving me a hug. Mrs. Williams has always been a great neighbor; she is in her seventies but never complained about any loud noise coming from our apartment. Jeremy had the best speakers money could buy set up in our living room and would loudly play back some of his mixes. You'd think the young DJ next door would get under the poor old lady's skin, but she always encouraged Jeremy and treated us like her grandkids.

"Yea, we broke up. I just wanted to stop by and say goodbye. I left on bad terms." I honestly divulge.

"Well Jeremy doesn't live here anymore either, Honey. He moved out about a month ago. He told me he bought himself one of those big houses they just built in uptown Tooley." She updates me.

"The new houses on Dark Ward Avenue?" I ask in shock.

"Yep, those ones." She confirms.

"Wow, he must be doing really well for himself." I say quietly more to myself.

"He really is… got him a great job at that new radio station. Go get that man, Britney. Don't let that one go." She says seriously. I smile but inwardly I am sick to my stomach. What if I never get to have him again? What if he's moved out and now lives with some other woman in a brand new, big house? Anthony Johnson only took six months to meet and marry someone after the two of us broke up; hopefully the same isn't true for Jeremy.

"Well thanks Mrs. Williams, I got to get back to school." I say somberly.

"Cheer up Britney. The Lord is always working, if

he's yours, he'll come back." She says as she locks her own apartment door and walks with me out of the building.

The bus ride back to school is somber. I decide against going to get my number changed incase Jeremy ever tried to contact me. Suddenly my phone rings, my heart jumps and I'm praying its Jeremy… but it isn't; it's Anthony from English class.

"Hello?" I answer sounding a little low spirited.

"Hey… Before you yell at me PLEASE don't hate me. I can't make it at 7 there's some mandatory partying I have to do tonight." He laughs psychotically.

"I KNEW IT!" I yell extremely annoyed I put myself in this damn predicament by accepting to be this joke's partner.

"Don't be mad, we'll get it done, I promise. Just come to the party with me tonight." He jokes.

"No. I'm still going to the Library tonight on my own after my math class. Unlike you, I take my grades seriously." I take the phone away from my ear and I'm close to hanging up when I hear him pleading on the other end.

"Wait, wait, wait… Look, come to my apartment on Sunday and we can knock out the whole project, I promise. I will do whatever it takes and we will work all night, it's just the weekend is my fun time." He admits.

"Fine." I decide to give him one more chance.

"Good girl, I'll text you my address. See you Sunday at like 4PM."

"Okay." I say skeptically.

"Cool." He croons.

"Bye Anthony."

"Bye Britney. ***click***"

Chapter 21: Extrasensory Perception

~2001 Present Day~

I wake up feeling sick to my stomach, it's Sunday *'the Sabbath'* but I'm not feeling the presence of God in my life at the moment. I am the most depressed I've even been in my entire life. All I've been able to think about for the past two nights is Jeremy and everything I've lost in the past year. What if he's gone forever? What if I never see him again? What if my life never gets back to the way it once was? The lump in my throat feels excruciating, so much so I have no desire to even live right now. Every decision I have ever made has ended up being a terrible one, I feel so lost and I don't know where to begin in finding myself again.

My alarm clock goes off and it triggers the radio to start playing. I'm guessing because it's a Sunday there's a quick fifteen-minute sermon on. It's a famous TV evangelist and you'll never guess what his quick sermon is about; redemption. "We've all done wrong, no one is without sin. Are you going to stay in bed this morning and dwell in the past, or are you going to get up, head to church, and begin a new chapter in your life? C'mon now! The world was against Jesus, THEY CRUCIFIED HIM! No hole you could possibly be in is close to the trouble Jesus was exposed to. I'm here with a message today, I'm here to tell you Jesus rose again and so will you, I'm here this morning, not by accident, but by Christ, to tell you to GET OUT OF BED, shake the depression off, because HE LIVES… and HE FORGIVES." I start to cry, this sermon was on point with what I was going through, either I had ESP or Jesus Himself was trying to send me a message.

Reluctantly, I decide to get out of bed and get on my knees and pray. "Dear Heavenly Father, I have ZERO idea what I'm doing in my life. I keep messing up… Where do I even start? I quit a great job and I still don't know if it was the right thing to do. I lost my fiancé, car, and apartment in the same month. I'm doing okay in English class, but I've been struggling in all my other classes. Life is so hard right now." I

174

start to cry. "I feel like a failure; I feel like I'm easily replaceable. I've had the same number and Jeremy still hasn't attempted to contact me... not once. He's not returning any of my calls and I have a feeling he's moved on. The law firm I worked in moved on pretty quickly as well... Like really? They hired a bar tender with no experience to replace me! I just feel unappreciated I just-" Before I can even finish my prayer, my phone rings. It's Bill Hogan. I am extremely surprised, not only was I JUST praying about the whole work situation, but I haven't heard from him since the voicemail he left on my phone the day I quit.

"Hello?" I answer my phone.

"Britney..." Hogan sighs, "Look, I know I wasn't always a good man *or boss* to you, but I'm going to cut to the chase... We really, really need you here." Wow, is Mr. Everyone-is-replaceable begging for me to come back and work for him? My self-worth was at an all-time low and now he calls out of the blue basically reassuring the fact that I am not only wanted, but needed. I definitely have ESP.

"I heard you replaced me though..." I began.

"With who? The blonde bartending bitch? I fired her on her third day. She was TERRIBLE. Britney, nobody is as proficient as you. I even tried pulling other secretaries from other lawyers, but they don't do as they're told without asking tons of prying questions. You never asked any questions, you just did your job and did it well." He went on. He is right, there were a lot of questionable cases I had to file throughout my four years with the firm, but I figured as successful as they were, and as educated as they were, they knew better than I did about law. So I just did what I was told, made my money, and went on with my business.

"Look, Bill."

"At least you called me Bill." He laughs, attempting to strike up memories and make light of the situation.

"Mr. Hogan, I loved how prestigious I felt while working for your firm, but after DC I learned there was way more to life than status. I want to make my own way. I am not interested in law, I don't get along with the other people your

175

firm has employed, and I have a lot going on in my own life right now as it is… Not to mention I *just* enrolled in school." I explain.

"One hundred and twenty thousand dollars… Quit school, come back to work for me, and I'll give you another advance. Also I'll never hold it over your head about how you abandoned ship." He barters with me. The last time I made a deal with Hogan I left my soul in the District of Columbia but honestly, this offer is sounding amazing. I take a long while to think things over in silence and this time I am actually extremely close to accepting his offer… Until he adds, "It's because I stopped fucking you isn't it? You bitches are always putting dick and emotions over money. Dumb as fuck. Can't a man in my position just get a nut without y'all going crazy? I thought you were different and all about advancing in corporate America. You had so much fucking potential; I was so close to forging a law degree for you and making you a damn millionaire lawyer." He barks out of nowhere. *What?* Did he just say he was close to forging a law degree for me?

"Mr. Hogan, it's Sunday so I'm not going to curse you out like I want to, but I will say this; I was going to consider your offer until you went belligerent and reminded me of why I never want to step foot in that evil building again. Take your job, the 120k you tried to bribe me with, and your dick, and get out of my life. NO DEAL! That place contributed in ruining my life and right now I'm focused on building it back up. I am finally finding my happiness and it started with getting as far away as possible from people like you. Don't ever call me back again, GOODBYE!" I hang up the phone. I feel empowered and amazing. If there's a God, this must be what He wants for my life. Things are just falling into place. I almost made the mistake of going back to work for that demon when he flipped out on his own, revealing his true colors. I really must have some sort of superpower.

I get off my knees and go take a shower and get ready for church, even though it's only 8AM and church doesn't start until 11am. My mother hasn't even woken up yet. Finally, an hour passes and I hear my mother getting out of bed, singing praises and hymns, and jumping in the shower. I sit patiently in my room, fully dressed and waiting silently to surprise her. At 10am I hear her walking down the stairs and yell up to me "I'M ON MY WAY TO CHURCH BRIT, SEE YOU IN A LITTLE BIT!" When I first moved back in with her she pestered me nonstop to attend church with her. She stopped inviting me after weeks of me rejecting her invitation and just spending Sunday's in my room sleeping in. Today as soon as she opens up the front door I run to her, fully dressed in my Sunday attire.

"Wait up, Ma." I smile at her as I beat her out the door. I can see the shock in her eyes. I can tell she is extremely touched. We go to the bus stop together, and for the first time in a long time I can see pride for her daughter in my mother's eyes.

We finally arrive at the church my mother has been attending since my father passed away with fifteen minutes to spare before the service begins. I remember being dragged here as a child for years. I haven't been inside of a church since I moved out of my mother's house and got an apartment with Jeremy. I think to myself, *if the pastor does a sermon on rebuilding. I definitely have ESP* as I follow my mother to the same pew she's sat in for years. My heart stops when I notice Ms. Jackson, my mother's neighbor is seated directly behind me. She gets up and greets my mother but doesn't even look in my direction. I feel like the devil for even being in this holy place. Finally, it's 11AM and the choir starts to sing, I'm going to need this service to go by fast... I can almost feel Mrs. Jackson's hatred searing through the back of my head.

I can't concentrate on any of the praising going on, I am too nervous thinking about whether or not I would get swung on, mid-sermon. Finally, 11:30AM reaches and the pastor is on the pew. His sermon is beautiful and tugs at my heart. So far it has nothing to do with rebuilding, but rather accepting responsibility and admitting fault. "You see we as Christians hide behind the word SIN too much" The pastor preaches. "'I can't help that I did that, we are all *sinners*', 'I can't stop *sinning*, I'm not Jesus, I'm only human', I could go on and on. Eve bit the apple intentionally; the devil didn't force it down her throat! Maybe if she would have just turned around and admitted her guilt instead of placing the blame on the snake, we would all still be in the Garden of Eden. Yes, we are all human, and yes we were born with the sins of our father's... BUT DON'T USE THAT AS AN EXCUSE BROTHERS AND SISTERS, because we have something Eve didn't have... We have strength and salvation through accepting the sacrifice of Jesus Christ."   Wow, I really feel like the sermon is urging me to apologize to Mrs. Jackson. I really feel the need to finally speak to her no matter how mad she is at me. My ESP was telling me this was the way to go. Once I start thinking of what I would say to her when I get the chance, the pastor switches up his message and begins to preach about rebuilding!

That's verification upon verification. It's like the universe has been ordering my steps since I woke up this morning. After the sermon ends, everyone is released to the recreation area to enjoy some snacks and beverages. I watch Mrs. Jackson walk towards a women's restroom and take that as an opportunity to speak to her in private. I wait about five minutes and then go in after her.

By the time I enter the restroom Mrs. Jackson is washing her hands, we make brief eye contact before she continues to ignore me, trying her hardest to act as though she didn't see me standing next to her. I make the moment even more awkward by walking up close to her.

"I know you hate me, you don't have to say anything back, but can you please just hear me out." I begin. "It's been almost six years since we last spoke--"

"Since you last DESTROYED my family." She snarls.

"Yes," I admit fault. "Since I last destroyed your family." I look down, nerves now getting the best of me, I dig deep and just let out the most honest words that come to mind. "I don't know what broke me, whether it was the loss of my father or the loss of what I thought was my first real love, but

178

I've been acting like a slut since I turned nineteen." I smile attempting to bring some humor into the very decrepit conversation.

"Don't go making excuses for what you did. You know damn well what you were doing, and I'm not sure what the hell this is, but I am nowhere near ready to have this conversation with you and I might never be." She barks.

"I know," I begin to cry. "I know I ruined your life. You think I feel good about who or what I am? My actions have cost me Jeremy; I don't have anyone now. I deserve this loneliness, but I'm mature now. Plus, after the pastor's message I thought I should attempt an apology. I did a despicable thing, I used to crave attention from men, I don't know why I did some of the things I did… I don't even know how to apologize to you without hating myself with every word that escapes my lips. I just know if I could take it all back, I would. I wish I didn't ruin your relationship; I wish I was a better person. All I can say is that moving forward I will be… and I want to do whatever it takes to get you to tolerate me again." At this point my face is red, puffy, and tears begin flowing down my cheeks. After what feels like an eternity, Mrs. Jackson finally responds.

"First of all Lil' Mama, *you* didn't ruin anything. For Deon to have fucked a little girl he basically helped raise was fucked up in itself. He did that ALL by himself. You helped me dodge a bullet, I would have been with him now not knowing what other shit he was doing behind my back." Her eyes are red and her voice cracks, but she doesn't cry. "As far as me forgiving you or us having any sort of relationship, I'm going to have to say ABSOLUTELY NOT. It is taking all that is in me not to strangle you right now…" I am a bit frightened after she says this. Mrs. Jackson has gained a lot of weight over the past six years and she could end my life with one good swing of her arm.

"I-I'm sorr--" I start.

"No, don't say ANYTHING! You are UNFORGIVEN! But I'll tell you what little Miss Britney, I don't forgive you, but I respect you. Coming in here after me

179

trying to right your wrong is commendable. That's all I'll say, and that's how we'll leave it. I know I'm a Christian and supposed to forgive, especially since we're in church and all, but I just can't. I can't forgive you and I can't forgive him. I've been the laughing stock of Dumois ever since my ex-husband fucked you right outside of my house in front of *everyone*, and I plan to take that misery with me to my grave. Now if you'll excuse me, I have to go." She walks towards the napkin dispensary and pulls a couple plies out then walks back towards me, handing them to me. "Clean yourself up." She says before exiting the restroom leaving me to cry alone. Even though she doesn't forgive me I feel like a big weight has been lifted from my shoulders… In some sick way I was finally at peace.

After taking about four buses, I finally arrive at Anthony's *(the one from English class)* apartment. He lives in Rosters, an apartment building located deep in Tooley, about an hour from Dumois, not too far from Hogan & Wildes. The building is a lot nicer than the Tooley Towne apartments I used to live in; it was just built about a year ago. The fact that he lives here tells me that he has rich parents, because there's no way someone without a decent paying job can afford a place like this.

He meets me at the entrance and greats the doorman

as we walk along the polished, marble floors. "Thanks for not cutting my head off about standing you up on Friday." He laughs as he unlocks his occupancy.

"Yea, I'm okay as long as we get this project done by Wednesday." I respond seriously.

"Lighten up." He jokes as he walks me into his studio apartment. It looks really junky… He has laundry lying everywhere. I had never been in a studio apartment before, although it was more spacious than the one-bedroom apartment I had with Jeremy, it had no rooms. The bed, dining room, and couch are all in the same room. "Make yourself at home, there's no room on the couch because of my clothes, but you can find a space on my bed." He laughs, "That is where all the magic happens!" Uncomfortable I just shift some clothes around on the couch and decide to sit there instead.

"So… Here's my part." I say while reaching in my bag and retrieving a binder full of research and notes I had worked on the night before. "This should make the process a lot easier, how about you? Where's your half?"

"Dang… You're just getting straight to the point, huh? Don't you want something to drink before we start?"

"Do you have any juice?" I ask.

"I meant like alcohol… This is a bachelor pad babe; I only have tap water and alcohol." He laughs.

"I'm okay, look… Let's just get to work, I got to wake up early tomorrow and I want to get this done."

"Okay." He says and then sits next to me.

"Okay, well this is what I was thinking, we write in first person the entire project and then at the end we reveal that the narrator is in fact the killer." I jump right in to school work.

"That sounds great." Anthony says so close to my neck, making me very uncomfortable.

"Can I see what you've done?" I ask one more time.

"I didn't do anything yet; I've been high all weekend." He busts out laughing. At this point I am done; I begin to hastily pack up my books and get up to leave.

Anthony quickly reaches for my ass when I get up. "Damn baby, so soft." I slap his hand away.

"Listen you disgusting, lazy ass pig," Anthony is shocked by my anger; he is really handsome and is probably used to women throwing themselves at him. Like I said before, maybe last year I would have fallen for his bullshit, but today I wasn't about any games. Education and getting my life back took precedence over everything. "If you EVER put your hands on me again I'll kill you. Now I don't know why the hell you brought me here but if you're going to just waste my time and play games and not do any damn work I'm going to leave."

"Alright, alright… Let's get to work." Anthony caves in so I sit back down. We spend the next three hours silently working. We successfully finish the paper and I get up to leave.

"Thank you Anthony, see you tomorrow in class." I say as I get up and walk out of his apartment without even waiting for a response. As I'm walking to the bus stop I am proud of myself. I am proud for staying strong and doing the right thing all day today. This has to be the beginning of a great life. I am optimistic and full of hope.

Since I have a long bus ride home I decide to tie up one last loose end. I decide to call Anthony Johnson, the original Anthony and give him a piece of my mind since I am on such a
roll today. The phone rings twice before I hear someone pick up.

"Don't say a word," I begin without even letting him speak. "This is Britney Greene, the girl you used to toy with. I want you to listen to everything I have to say and then I promise to delete your number for good. You fucking turned me into a heartless girl and for years I've felt messed up since we broke up. I was nothing but nice to you and I really feel like you took advantage of me. Well despite everything you've done, I want you to know I don't hate you anymore. I am a new and improved woman and in a sick way I want to thank you, because had you not fucked me up emotionally I wouldn't have become the strong individual I am today. I don't blame you for decisions I've made after you, but you do have a part in fucking up my self-esteem causing me to act out in ways I otherwise never would have. I wish nothing but the best for you and your family; I just hope you start treating your wife better than you treated me. The last time we saw each other you tried to fuck me and she doesn't deserve that. Women are not fucking instruments you play with; we weren't created for you to take advantage of. Please get help." I let out in one breath. I start smiling because this was everything I had wanted to tell him for years. Just when I was about to hang up the phone I hear a voice that makes my stomach turn:

"This Tina, not Anthony. I am his wife. And please don't ever worry about how he's treating me, because unlike you I don't play the victim. I kicked Anthony's ass out days ago and I have his cell phone because he bought it with my father's money. Out of all the women that have called for him since I've had his phone in my possession, you sweetheart are the funniest. Stop being so pathetic calling a married man to air out your personal issues. Bye! ***click*"** I laugh hysterically… Well at least that settles it… I don't have extrasensory perception; otherwise I would have seen that coming. Regardless of how much of a fail that phone call was, I truly feel like this whole day has been getting a lot of baggage off my shoulders. I am finally free of pain and full of forgiveness and I know who I am and who I want to be. Finally, my future looks bright and I honestly feel that I owe it all to one man… Jesus.

Chapter 22: Serendipity

~2002 Present Day~

Two years pass since I started school and it is a couple of months past my twenty-ninth birthday, I am walking across a stage in my school's auditorium to accept my Associate's degree in communications.

"Britney Greene." My name is finally called and I can hear my mother shouting in the audience before I can see her. It has taken a lot to finally get here; that kind of strength could have only came from the Lord. I've abstained from a lot more than just sex during these past two years, I've avoided men with cruel intentions, I gave up countless nights I could have gone out and partied in order to focus on studying, and today… It all paid off. A week before I was set to walk the stage I accepted a job offer with The Tooley Times, the starting salary wasn't as big as what I was getting at Hogan & Wildes, but it truly is a great start. I will finally be able to move my mother and myself into a house in Tooley, I'll also be able to buy myself a car again, but this time I'm looking into getting something more practical.

When I get off the stage I am greeted by my mother and tears of joy are streaming down her face. She is so beautiful and is about to make me cry. She has been my rock for the past couple of years. She worked double shifts at the restaurant in order to help support me going back to school full time and now with my stable job and salary she'll be able to quit her own job and retire. I pull her in extremely close as we make our way back to our seats.

"I have a surprise for you after the ceremony." She smiles maliciously.

"Okay..." I say feeling both partly suspicious and excited... what is this woman up to? I laugh to myself.

The speaker at my graduation grew up in Dumois and is now one of the biggest real estate moguls in Tooley; he is very motivational and funny. I made the decision to further my education, which would help me move up in ranks at the paper. A bachelor's degree would be a good thing to fall back on if God forbid, I ever lose a job again. I plan to go to a four-year college but only part time as I work full time at the paper until that degree is acquired.

The ceremony is finally over and I meet my mother in the hallway after everyone is dismissed.

"What's the surprise?" I laugh, anxious to be in on her secret.

"It's behind you walking this way." She smiles ever so sweetly. I immediately turn around and walking in my direction is Jeremy Rogers, my ex. I drop my diploma and everything else I have in my hands. My mother picks them up for me and gives me a little nudge to move towards Jeremy. "I'll be waiting by the entrance, come out whenever you're done." She smirks as she carries all my stuff out with her.

"Hi." Jeremy says as he approaches me. My heart sinks, I don't know whether I am overwhelmed with heartbreak or happiness, but nevertheless I begin balling irrepressibly.

"Where have you been?" I sob. "I've been looking for you for two years."

"I needed time, Brit. It was a lot. I was in my own world for a while, depressed." He admits.

"How'd you know I was graduating? Like, how'd you find me?" I ask in between sniffles.

"Your mother set this up; this is *ALL* Ms. Greene's doing" He smiles. "Please don't cry... I don't like it when you

185

cry." He says as he reels me into his arms. Am I dreaming? "Your mother called me about a year ago and told me she really saw a change in you. For that to come from *her*, I took it seriously." He was right; my mother was never my biggest fan in the past, so for her to notice a change in my behavior and contact Jeremy on my behalf said a lot.

"... But I tried calling you for years and you didn't pick up!" I sniffle. "I thought you changed your number."

"No, I was mad at you so I blocked you and I made sure I didn't answer any unknown numbers. I couldn't bear seeing you or hearing from you; I would have either taken you back prematurely or lashed out at you... but when your mother contacted me, I couldn't disrespect her by ignoring her. Despite what you and I go through, she's been like a mother to me... so I picked up her call. Truth be told, I'm glad I did." He laughs.

"So what now?" I say getting ahead of myself. Jeremy looks down at his shoes before responding.

"I don't know." As soon as those three words leave his lips, I break down. I've been waiting years to finally be face to face with this man, and now that I am I don't ever want to let him out of my sight again.

"Jeremy, I *have* changed. I am in a better place, I'm stronger, I'm saner, I've got my emotions in check... The only thing that hasn't changed about me is the fact that I'm still madly in love with you. I know I hurt you baby, but I hurt myself as well. The life I was living was going to have me end up just like my father. I don't want that for myself, I want what I used to have; your love. None of those other guys even compare to you. I haven't been on one single date since you left me. I was really about to just give up on men entirely and just be single for the rest of my life like my mother, but I always kept you in my prayers. I didn't only pray that you would forgive me, but I prayed for you to achieve whatever you desired in life and I prayed that you found love again, even if it wasn't with me. I remember you saying you just wanted to be enough Jer. I remember when you told me that, and I'm standing here today telling you, YOU ARE

ENOUGH! YOU WERE ALWAYS ENOUGH! I just didn't see it back then." I start crying again. Jeremy suddenly lets his walls fall down and takes me deeper into his arms.

"That's all I wanted to hear." He breathes a sigh of relief. Without notice he gets on one knee. "I thought I'd make this day even more special for you." He smiles as he reaches in his pants' pocket and retrieves a little box.

"Oh my God." I gasp as a crowd begins to form around us.

"Britney Greene, the truth is I've been just as miserable without you. Both our lives seem to be moving in a successful direction, you graduating, me getting promoted at the radio station, but what are accomplishments like those without having that one person to share them with? Britney, you are my one person. I haven't so much as touched another woman since you and I broke it off and I swear on it. I was just waiting for you to finally want me as much as I've always wanted you. I've been watching your growth from a distance and I am really proud of you. Please make me even more proud by being my wife." He opens the box and it's the same ring I saw the last day I was in our apartment… I am flattered he kept it for all this time. It's even more beautiful than I remembered. The fact that he kept the ring is a sign that he never really gave up on me but was just waiting for me to grow up emotionally. Truth is, I needed that tough love because had he taken me back sooner, I probably would have taken advantage of him again and not learned my lesson.

"Yes!" I screech as he places the ring on my finger and gets up and embraces me, lifting me in the air. This truly is the happiest day of my life. The onlookers clap and random strangers come up to us and congratulate our milestone. Jeremy and I make our way outside where we meet up with my mother; she is equally excited when she sees the ring on my finger.

"THANK YOU JESUS!" She exclaims, "I've been praying for this!"

~Weeks Later~

Jeremy and I are out on a romantic date at one of Tooley's fairly new, yet highly acclaimed restaurants. We are privately celebrating our engagement and rekindled love. We had a big engagement party at his house last weekend, and it was jam packed with loved ones. Both of our families and most of his co-workers were in attendance. That same week I moved from my mother's house into his nice three story home, which is located about an hour away from where we used to live. It's in a new gated community in uptown Tooley and I must say I am *very* proud of my fiancé. Not only is he doing great as the music director for TXA, but his own business, Bells Will Be Ringing, LLC has grown tremendously in the two years we were apart. He now has about fourteen employees working under him, and one of them was even the DJ at our engagement party. He has two great incomes coming at him year round and he is my motivation to work harder in life. Not only have I decided to continue my education part time and work for the paper full time, but I am currently brainstorming a motivational book/autobiography about the ups and downs I've encountered in life and how I've overcame a lot of obstacles.

Dinner is going great but we can't seem to keep our eyes off of each other. The electricity between us is even stronger than when we first met and started dating. Since we got back together, Jeremy and I made the decision not be intimate until our wedding night and the lack of sex has filled us with built up desires. God has been good in both our lives and abstaining is one of the ways we want to honor him for being gracious to us even though we haven't always deserved His mercy. We both can hardly wait to say "I do"; I honestly think we're going to have sex in the limo ride immediately following our ceremony. Anyways, the food is amazing and everything is fairytale-like… That is, until I spot two people I never dreamed I would ever see again being seated at a table adjacent to us.

Jeremy sees the shock in my face. "What's wrong?" He asks concerned.

"That's Jane and Greg." I whisper.

"Oh." He rolls his eyes. "Look, we're here to have a good time and leave the past in the past. Don't let the sight of them take your joy, hell, go say hi to them if you want." He laughs attempting to lighten the mood. Jeremy knows exactly who Greg and Jane are. We've been talking a lot since we've gotten back together; we've even attended a premarital course with our church where I've filled him in on every sex-scapade of mine. He knows Greg was the last man I slept with other than him and he knows Greg is the reason he found a condom wrapper in our bedroom. I do a quick glance in their direction just to make sure it's really them... It is. Jane is peering back at me with a menacing grin. She begins running her fingers through Greg's newly cut Mohawk just to add to the dramatics. I know who *hasn't* matured in over two years.

When we finish our meal, Jeremy puts down a tip for our waitress as we get up to leave. On our way out of the restaurant Jane calls out for me.

"Oh Brit Brit... So you're really just going to act like you don't see us here?" She snarls. I stop in my tracks and make the decision to swing by their table.

"You want me to come with you?" Jeremy asks, looking a little annoyed by Jane's antics.

"No baby, I got this." I say giving him an assuring kiss.

"Ok, I'll be in the car. Text me if you need me to come back in here and whoop some ass." He jokes. I laugh and watch him leave the restaurant before turning around and going back in Jane and Greg's direction.

"Hi." I say innocently, refusing to react to Jane's initial rude ass remark. "I saw you guys enjoying an intimate dinner and I didn't want to impose, but there's no bad blood here. It was really nice seeing you guys again." I am attempting to exude cordiality.

"We haven't seen you since you went crazy and quit the firm." Jane comments and they both laugh belligerently.

"Oh yea, I was in a bad place back then, and working there turned me into something I'm not proud of. If I ever did or said anything to offend either of you, I apologize." I say

189

honestly.

"Yea, yea, yea," Greg says. "It's all in the past now.... So was that Mr. Man?"

"Yes, that was my fiancé; Jeremy." I smile proudly.

"When's the wedding?" Jane coos sardonically.

"In a couple of months, but we just got back together recently, so the actual wedding plans aren't written in stone yet." I share.

"Ahh..." Jane voices judgmentally.

"Yea, but we're good now." I smile, again brushing off her negativity.

"Well, we just got engaged too." Jane brags showing me her ring. "And Greg has moved up and is now supervisor clerk of the mailroom; he got a raise and everything... Even has his own office!" She sings.

"Oh, congratulations." I smile.

"Yea, my ring isn't as big as yours, but you probably got that from leftover Hogan money, huh?" Jane scoffs.

"No. Actually Jeremy paid for it on his own, he works at the TXA radio station in town and has his own business, plus my Hogan money went into my education and helping my mother out with rent, so that's all gone now." I disclose.

"Education?" Greg inquires.

"Yea, I just graduated from Tooley Community College, and now I'm about to go work for The Tooley Times." I say proudly.

"The Tooley Times? Wow, you're okay about going from Hogan & Wildes to The Tooley Times?" Greg laughs.

"Yes, I love to write... so naturally journalism is right down my alley. I'm pretty sure I've told you that before." I respond.

"Congratulations!" Jane cuts in, "I think Greg is just shocked about how you're okay with going from a big time law firm to a small time paper." And with that, they both start to cackle. That was the last straw; I have been trying to be nice this entire conversation but I can feel them unleashing a side of me I have been trying my hardest to suppress.

"Nice seeing you guys again." I say abruptly and then

turn to leave, trying my best to prevent a disastrous confrontation.

"Bye, Small Time!" Greg yells after me while I'm almost out the door. That was it. I storm back to their table with a few last words.

"I know damn well you're not calling me 'small time' for going after my dreams instead of kissing ass working at a law firm I didn't like. Besides, the only thing *small time* here is in your pants!" I spew and then storm out of the restaurant. Before actually exiting I could hear Jane losing her mind.

"YOU TOLD ME Y'ALL DIDN'T DO ANYTHING!" She screamed.

"WE DIDN'T BABY!" He yelled back.

"THEN HOW IN THE HELL DOES SHE KNOW YOUR SIZE?" She screamed back. I am laughing hysterically on my way to the parking lot. As entertaining as it would have been to stand there and listen in on their entire argument, I had something much better waiting for me in a parked car.

"You okay?" Jeremy looks at me a little worried when I finally meet up with him.

"I'm great." I smile as I lean in for a kiss.

Good luck to Jane; thank God I dodged that bullet. Jeremy and I drive off laughing as I fill him in about what happened inside the restaurant after he left. After that day, I never see either Jane or Greg again.

Chapter 23: Olympus Has Fallen

~2005 Present Day~

I am sitting in my new office reflecting over the past three years of my life. I am now thirty-two years old and for the past two and a half years, I have legally been Mrs. Britney Rogers. Life is amazing and I can't complain. I am four months pregnant with my second child; her name is Emma, after my mother. My first child is a boy; his name is Kyle Rogers, after Jeremy's late brother. We are celebrating Kyle's second birthday in a couple of weeks. Jeremy and I are still going strong; we moved our family into a bigger house further west of Tooley. We bought it last summer when we found out we were having our second child. Conveniently this new house is only blocks away from my mother's house; they are both the same size and mansions in their own right. I bought my mother her house two years ago as a surprise for her Birthday... No more 'low incoming housing' Dumois for her.

My honeymoon was beautiful; Jeremy and I went to Jamaica and then spent a weekend in DC. Over the years we have been fairly well traveled; Ivory Coast, Panama, London, and Australia are just some of the places we've visited so far on vacation. Jeremy was invited to the Annual Business Gala for his work with turning the little TXA radio station into a major network heard across the nation. Bells Will Be Ringing, LLC is also a nationwide full service wedding contracting company where a couple can book everything from a DJ to a cinematographer. As for me, my book "When Life Gives You Lemons" made the top sellers list last year. It is a self-help book loosely based on my real life experiences. I get emails daily from people thanking me for sharing my story and motivating others who were raised in the slums, like Dumois, to continue pushing on and never giving up. Most of the money made from my book sales has gone to the charities Jeremy and I have started in an attempt to completely rejuvenate the city of Dumois. It's going to take a lot of work, time, and money, but we're hoping that in the next five years, visually and economically, one will no longer be able to tell the difference between Tooley and Dumois. Day by day, living conditions are improving, crime is reducing, and there's a stronger sense of community and hope, even in the people still living in public housing.

At this very moment I am sitting in my new enormous corner office, looking at my South African imported door with hand carved designs surrounding my gold overlaid name plate. It reads: Britney Rogers, *Editor in Chief*. That's right; I worked my way up to the top of The Tooley Times Paper. I started as a mere journalist years ago and now I'm in charge. Suddenly there's a knocking at my door.

"Come in." I declare.

"Hi Mrs. Rogers?" One of my new employees, Ana James enters timidly.

"Have a seat." I say politely.

"Thanks," She sits down adjacent to me. "I wanted to run a story by you to see if you liked it for the cover."

"Shoot." I smile at her. Ana was always coming into my office with great ideas, I saw a little bit of myself in her. This is what I did when I first started working here and now look where I'm at, I have no doubt she will one day make a great editor in chief.

"Okay, well, get this. I just got off the phone with an insider at the Tooley Police Station and apparently one of America's biggest law firms is getting shut down!" She sings, excited to be breaking this story. "Can you guess which one?"

"Hogan and Wildes?" I ask shocked.

"YES, the head honchos, the biggest celebrity attraction in Tooley, and not to mention one of the top five firms in North America!" She shrieks.

"I'm all ears." I say leaning in. This was incredible; I am impatiently waiting to hear the whole story.

"Okay, well... There's an insider, a former employee who is at the station right now working with the police. They have been talking to her for almost a year trying to build their case against the firm. Apparently it's all been a front and there are a lot of lawyers there that don't even have a legitimate law degree; William Hogan being one of them." I am shocked and listen intently as she continues. "The informant even has proof that they have been bribing certain judges in order to win cases over the years." She is speaking faster than my brain can compute all this astonishing information. "... AND, unrelated, William Hogan has just been slapped with a thirty-million-dollar law suit for sexual harassment by about four of his former employees. And they very well may have a strong case, especially with all the public speculation that he's slept with a lot of his employees throughout the years. I mean, he's already in all the blogs for being a womanizer so they have a strong case. One of the women is even claiming he drugged and raped her on a trip to DC!"

"Oh my God." I am stunned. In all my years of working at Hogan & Wildes I was only aware of the sexual corruption, I had no idea how big of a fraud William J. Hogan really was, and I'm pretty sure Evica is in on all of the scandal. "Do you know who the informant is?" I ask.

"Get this, her name is Louisa, she used to work for the company but quit years ago... *and* she is also the cousin of Evica Wildes! She has a sick vendetta with William Hogan and is claiming she was done wrongfully by him. She's willing to testify against everyone at the firm in court. My informant says she wanted to come back and work at H&W last year but Hogan didn't approve her return. This is what triggered her to blow the whistle on everything and initiate her liaison with police." I bust out laughing, I don't wish suffering on *anyone*, but this is Karma at its finest.

"I'm sorry." I stop laughing, "It's just... I used to work there and all this is overwhelming." I admit.

"Wow! I didn't know you worked at H&W... Do you think I can interview you for my story?" Ana asks surprised.

"Yea, why not." I laugh. "My life is an open book... *literally*."

"Oh is that the law firm you talked about in your book?" She laughs, finally putting two and two together. I changed the names of a lot of people and places in my manuscript in an attempt to avoid lawsuits. "My goodness, there was a lot of scandal going on over there." She cackles.

Ana has read my book and is just now figuring everything out. "Did you know Louisa?" She inquires.

"Yep, I was her subordinate turned replacement." I reveal.

"WOW!" Ana is so excited. "This story is going to be HUGE!"

"It sure is; it might even win you an award if you're the first to break it." I encourage her.

"Do you think you can get me an actual interview with Louisa?"

"I'll try." I laugh, "But I honestly think she hates me more than she hates Evica and Bill. I am the main reason she quit... but just go ahead and write up everything you can with the information you already have and I'll work on getting you a one on one with Louisa."

"Yes ma'am." Ana gets up to leave my office. I can't believe everyone at Hogan & Wildes, LLP; *the smuggest workforce in Missouri* are all going to be unemployed and under investigation in a matter of weeks... *allegedly* of course, if what Ana just told me was true. That just goes to show you that in life, nothing is certain. Always be grateful for what you have because it can be gone like the wind in a matter of moments. Also remain humble when moving up in life and never forget where you come from, because God can always send you back there. I learned both of those lessons years ago and I continue to live by them. Now it was their turn.

~Fin~

www.ingramcontent.com/pod-product-compliance
Lightning Source LLC
Chambersburg PA
CBHW031317120626
46554CB00001BA/442